Marcus Bird

AN ELEPHANT IN KINGSTON
AND OTHER STORIES

ISBN 978-0-9913239-3-7

"Do or do not. There is no try."

- Yoda, Jedi Master

CONTENTS

6

Alan

There was something about clocks that always felt like a fiddler's mad tune to me. The *tick* of each hand would blast into my ears, and I would squint my eyes slightly, trying to will time to slow, to keep myself in a world between the pauses during the seconds. The psychiatrist had mentioned that this was a delusion, and that people with *delusions* needed to attempt to accept reality. This was days after I confessed I wanted to kill myself, and that things hadn't had much meaning for a while for me. To this statement, the psychiatrist had barely reacted; his eyes still quiet and dark brown behind his lenses, the only noise in the office, the quiet humming of the air conditioner.

"What do you value?" he had said.

Value! I thought at the time. To me value is something inherent to a life of value, a causality of desires and wants that have been actualized or is in the process of actualization. The psychiatrist didn't agree. For him, the value in life was relative to wanting to live.

"Reasons, are like roots," he had said. "Roots that ground you when you feel as if you are in despair."

He said something else but I had lost time again, staring at the clock in his office, which was small and black, with the name *Zenith* printed in small bold gold letters above the number twelve. It became immediately apparent to me I had no idea Zenith made clocks. A quick mental note to do further research came to mind. After that session, I received a new prescription. Now I was taking some yellow ghastly tasting pills. My delusion pills.

The office is cold and outside the sky is bright and sunny. My fingers make a soft pattering noise on the desk as I keep watching the clock, I need to see Mr. Fitzroy, and I don't like Mr. Fitzroy. Mr. Fitzroy always came to work with a yellow mug that read " BEST DUDE EVER", dressed in expensive shirts doused in cologne that could have been pleasant if it wasn't a pungent cloud that clung to every artifact around him like an itinerant simian. Near the clock is a painting on the wall, a happy summer scene with tan people in orange swimwear. Now time really begins to slow, and I start to remember.

There was a time, when my mind was calm and things felt like the summer pool as a kid. My parents would take our next-door neighbour's son and me to their friend's house. They were the Watkins and the Watkins had a pool. The anticipation we had was amazingly fierce in its intensity; I could see the clear blue liquid of the pool in my eyes, smell something tasty cooking on the grill in the distance, and then hear my friend Gregory laughing in the car. On the trip to the Watkins' we would create epic battles with small action figures, scale the frozen caps of daunting mountains (this was represented by the car divider) and storm castles to save princesses. Every other weekend was devoted to this task, until one day, as we splashed about the pool, I noticed Gregory was still holding his breath underwater. I thought this was a herculean feat, because my lungs had burned for air moments before when I surfaced. At the time, I touched him and he didn't move, and I laughed, thinking he was doing some expert acting. Then terror hit my system as Gregory's father jumped into the pool fully clothed, and pulled him out of the water. He entered the pool badly, and scraped his elbow on one of the steps in the shallow end. The water in that area started to turn a cool pink from the blood oozing form his arm and the air filled with a chorus of loud adult voices filled with a shrill tension I would later recognize was fear.

Gregory was laid down at the side of the pool, his body an odd grey, quite different from its usual brown complexion. I marveled at his tenacity, even saying this to my father, who slapped me so hard in the face I lost a tooth. With pain throbbing in my jaw, I ran to the bathroom, crying in disbelief, spitting out blood for what seemed like an eternity. The muffled voices of the adults talking drifted through the air to where I was, and then came a soft, whimpering moan. It spread throughout the confines of the house like a low breeze, and then it turned into a roaring wail. I have never heard a sound like it since.

Wads of tissues were in my mouth, and I squinted in the bright sunlight when I stepped out of the bathroom. I saw Gregory's father holding his body, the small arms stiff and flapping about slightly like rubber. That was the first moment I felt time slow down; the fixed motion of impending Rigor Mortis with my friend, the broad, wet back of Gregory's father and his arm stained in blood where he had scraped his hand. It was all against the backdrop of a stark blue sky with soft cotton puff clouds rolling idly to their various destinations. I could also see my father's eyes, stained with tears and a flash of anger as he looked at me, standing still and wet, with the cotton in my mouth. It was painful to see, and I wanted it to vanish into the cold mountains we used to travel with our armies, but nothing changed, and the wailing went on for what seemed like forever. Now, Mr. Fitzroy.

I'm handing in a report to Fitzroy. He looks at me with a grunt, his round face shaved perfectly smooth, the contours of his nose slightly shiny. I could tell he wore Brooks Brothers shirts and Dockers pants today, because I shopped at the same Men's store. The office is quiet because a lot of the staff is off to some convention dealing with New Media. As usual, I declined the trip, saying I had to focus on a task of questionable importance.

Programming software is my talent. Several years before, I wrote code that laid some of the groundwork for online banking systems. Sheepish and skinny the day I rubbed shoulders with venture capitalists, I was already in a position to stay at home or lounge on the beach and do whatever I wanted. Sometimes, I thought about making video games, and I applied for a few positions in different companies, but then I would remember the days Gregory and I had made our imaginary worlds, and I would sometimes feel sad that I was doing the same thing again.

Idleness and boredom made me apply to my current position, a small tech firm paying me a ridiculously high salary for my services, even thought I don't need the money. A few sleazy up and comers in the office sometimes chatted about me, and I walked into the kitchen one day in mid-me talk.

"Y'know, we were wondering why you are here," a guy name Jeff said. "Aren't you like a millionaire? Shouldn't you be chasing bitches and sipping Pina Coladas on some beach?"

"I-I-m here because I want to be," I replied in a stutter.

The stutter came and went when I was nervous. Guys like Jeff made me uneasy. He was brash and confident, dripping with good looks and intelligence. Despite my own intelligence, it was hard for me to look into the eyes of people with so much *pizzazz*.

"If I was this guy," Jeff said to his friend. "I'd have my own company, an office building and a staff of twenty."

The coffee I came to make was ready, and I give Jeff a grim smile as I walk out. This subject of self-actualization had been broached with my psychiatrist as well, when I wondered out loud why I didn't invest my earnings from my software success.

"Many people fear success," the psychiatrist had said, his eyes crocodile-like behind his glasses. "Do you fear success?"

The answer was never clear. The day my father hit the tooth out of my mouth something changed. I was always trying to be alone. I feared the passage of time, and the way people eventually became *rubbery* and *grey*. I was obsessed with new worlds that had nothing to do with the real world. Experimenting with programming MODs (modifications) for obscure video games was my original past time, before I started dabbling in computer science and figured out my first few good pieces of software. A modification allowed me to take a piece of something and add something different to it. I could take a cityscape and add rivers and canyons, or turn a basement into a slithery alien dungeon. I'd smell these environments and atmospheres, wishing and imagining I was away from wherever I was. I didn't want to be in the world, but I was in it.

These days when I wasn't working, I had my video games, rife with Hollywood grade cinematic cut scenes, excellent voice acting and engaging stories that took days and days to finish. My setup for this escape was the ultimate in immersive tech. I preordered one of the first hundred-inch LCD televisions from Panasonic the day the model was announced. I had several gaming systems interlinked to the main unit, with surround speakers set up in a large room which doubled as the theatre.

"This," the real estate agent had said to me, "Is one of the true value points of this property. It is an escape, with its own garden, pool, and stone cut wine cellar."

I agreed with him it was a find. The pool was somewhat of a test. I hadn't been in one since I was a child, and some days I would go outside and sit on the lawn chairs, looking at the serene, unmoving surface of the water, but I couldn't go in. A memory of myself and Gregory in the Watkins' pool would come to mind, then fear would clutch me and I'd go back inside the house.

The day at the office is winding down, and I'm seeing the orange-red hue of sunset spill over the city. I haven't told my psychiatrist, but I feel like killing myself again. The yellow pills aren't helping so much, and the days still feel like a blur. The clocks around me have started to become my enemies, and even my escape into the world of games isn't enough.

I pop the top button of my Brooks Brothers shirt and blast the air conditioning in the car on the drive home. I love the *ssssh* coming from the air vents. This will probably be something I will miss (if one can miss something after death) because it was the deciding factor for me when I bought this S.U.V. Now it doesn't matter so much, and I hear an old Aerosmith song blare on the radio as the traffic lights fly by in a stream.

The plan is to consume this entire bottle of pills, with some alcohol for added effect. I see my property come into view, the sleek, serrated rooftop with pine lining (the real estate agent had emphasized this), Spanish style walls with the outcropping of plants grown on the gate. After pulling into the driveway, I sit in the car for a moment, playfully sucking in the Freon-laced air conditioner air.

The house greets me with its usual yawn. *The cleaning lady came today*, I remember. I take out a few hundred from my wallet, slip it into a blank envelope from my home office and write "Marta" on the front. A bird squawks outside somewhere, and I twiddle my thumbs briefly, wondering what to write. *Thanks for the good work*, I scribble. That seems fine.

The house is normally quiet, unless I am playing games in front of the television. Today, I'm blasting an old 90's hip-hop mix streaming from YouTube on my laptop, but I don't listen to hip-hop. The Brooks Brothers shirt is now open by four buttons and I have a few bottles of choice liquor on the kitchen counter. Grey Goose, Patron, Smirnoff Vodka and beers. The music is roaring in my ears, but I still can't feel much. The psychiatrist previously explained to me that I was searching for a *stimulus,* or *stimuli* or something like that. I try to work up a sweat by waving my arms, but nothing happens. The music isn't bad though; the 90's seemed like good times.

Four of the pills are in the palm of my hand, and they go down my throat in a burning chorus with a shot of Grey Goose. I take a beer from a six-pack case and chug it, feeling a quick lightness in my forehead. The music seems to be louder and more insistent now, the lyrics dull, but the snares, high hats and kicks clear as bells.

Another sip of Grey Goose and the world starts to feel like the engine of my luxury car, precise and formulaic. I start to think about the parallels between tribal societies and metropolitan societies, and drift to the balcony. The crescendo of my despair hits my chest with an oddly cold feeling; the music and the pills are making everything darker and quieter. There are now ten or so pills in my left palm, another glass of Grey Goose in my right. I think *No Diggity* is playing in the mix now. I smile because I actually know that song. I raise the pills to my mouth, and pause. There is someone on my lawn.

It shouldn't matter, my mind says. *Maybe he's the drifter who'll report you dead before the stink of your body after two weeks starts bothering the neighbours.*

My hand remains at my mouth for a few moments, slightly trembling. I lower it.

"Hey man," I say.

The fellow has his back turned and is staring towards the night sky. He is tall, wearing a large grey shirt and oversized khaki shorts.

"Hey man!" I shout.

The fellow moves his head slightly, as if acknowledging that he heard me. Oddness about his body language makes me curious, as if his movements alone were communicating to me. Curiosity turns into indignation.

"Listen, if you don't get off my lawn, I'm calling the cops!" I shout.

Inside, my suicidal mind makes a grisly smile. *Good, soon he'll be gone, and we can finish business,* I hear it say. The man turns around, smiles, and everything changes. Something is flowing from him; purity held in the calm intensity of his gaze, the startling symmetry of his face, and mostly his eyes. Even thirty feet away, something in them makes me almost completely sober.

"A day apart, a day at rest, this is what makes us the best," the man says.

I freeze, my blood cold.

"A day apart, a day at rest! This is what makes us the best!" he says, beaming the same electric smile.

I step back from the balcony. I can hear the pills clatter to the ground, and the dull crash of the glass I was holding hit the tiled floor. The balcony swims in my vision, and then I'm at home again, as a little boy, with my father towering over me. It was on a day when he wasn't particularly grumpy, and was telling me about work ethic.

"My father always had something he said to me," my father had said in a gravelly baritone. "He would say, 'A day apart, a day at rest, this is what makes us the best.' Now you say it son."

At the time, I repeated the phrase with youthful gusto, even waving my arms and patting my chest as I did it. My father had laughed at the time (a rare event) and gave me a hug (even rarer). I had never told anyone about this moment. My vision swam again, and I was back on the balcony. The man was still standing on the lawn looking up at the sky.

"Beautiful isn't it?" he says.

A slight fogginess is in my head, but I look up. Indeed it was an unusually bright evening. Twilight is turning into night and the purple black sky is dotted with shards of white.

"It's like we spend all this time in our little cubbyholes, digging away for our lives, but we forget that we have this over our heads all the time," the man says.

I confirm there is definitely something strange about our communication. The man is not close to the balcony by any means, nor is he shouting, but I can hear everything he says crystal clear, as if a transmitter was attached to my ears, amplifying his words. Something about his voice is soothing and relaxing.

"Looks like you are done with your cubbyhole," the man says.

He walks closer to the balcony, until he is almost under it.

"Are you done with it all?" he asks.

"I-I don't know," I reply, unaware of why I was answering this stranger.

Being dressed in a baggy shirt and oversized shorts didn't seem to make him an odd character. The clothes seemed to be a simple extension of whatever energy he was exuding. I could imagine him anywhere in these clothes, fitting in perfectly.

"No sense being done yet," the stranger says, staring directly at me.

I cannot hold his gaze. There is a magnetism he emits that hits my skull like rubber coated nails. Looking at my left arm, I see it is trembling slightly. I worried to myself, was this another delusion? Had I taken another step into true darkness?

"You aren't crazy," the man replies calmly.

A quick fright floods my system. *How did he*—then the feelings washes into a chilling calm. We stand there for a few moments and I realize my fogginess is gone. In fact, I feel like I'd had no trace of alcohol that evening.

"You want a drink?" I ask.

"Why not," the man replies.

He is quite tall, almost a head taller than me. I can see he had a lean, athletic build hidden beneath the folds of his baggy clothing. Casually, he stands dead center in the mansion's entrance hallway and surveys the inside of the house. He looks around with a slight smile on his face. There is no judgment in this activity, just simple evaluation. I can tell he is a man who had seen many things.

"Nice digs," he says.

He walks towards the entertainment room, and lets out a noise of delight.

"NO WAY!" he bellows, grabbing a few game cartridges from a shelf beside my television in his hand. "I love these games!"

The games he raved about were from the 80's, a collection of old Nintendo classics that I had purchased at an auction. The man sits on the ground, looking at the boxes and reading the information about them on the back of the display cases. He mumbles something about the Legend of Zelda game, and then laughs when he sees my Nintendo Metroid cartridge.

"I used to love playing these," he remarks.

Again, I notice I hear exactly what he says with absolute clarity, even though I am standing in the kitchen and he is by the television about twenty feet away. Quickly, I make another drink.

"Do you know the best part about these games?" the man asks.

"I'm not sure, I guess it's open to speculation," I reply.

"Nah man, it's the duality in all of them. These games, these stories, these missions all have one general contrast between good and evil. You battle for a worthy cause, you brave the elements to reach a point that makes you *feel* something."

"In some games you are the villain though," I say.

"Exactly! Even if you are a villain, you are against the *other* side, fitting into the duality. You can't have a game with only good characters, or a game with totally evil characters, it just doesn't equate. Even in games like Super Mario, with chestnut castles and magic mushrooms, you still had dudes throwing hammers at your head!"

After saying this, he laughs, a laugh that fills the entire house. It echoes everywhere at once, and I feel warmth briefly fill my body as a groundswell of good feeling rushes through my blood. He keeps laughing, and without realizing it, I am laughing too.

"So cubbyholes," the man says.

His face becomes serious, and the magnetic eyes pierce me once more.

"You don't want to dig anymore do you?" he asks.

"I don't know what you are talking about," I reply.

The man sighs briefly and sits on one of the couches facing the television. He is a little too tall for the small couch, and rests his feet on a nearby Ottoman.

"When a dog is ready to die, do you know what it does?" the man asks.

"A dog? What are you talking about?" I reply.

"A dog. When it is ready to die. Most animals in fact. When they get badly injured or sick, and they know the end is coming, do you know what they do?"

"Enlighten me."

"They crawl or hobble to the deepest darkest place they can find, and lay down and expire."

He didn't say anything else, and I stood there, with the drink in my hand, watching him stare at everything and nothing.

"I don't get what you—"

"YOU AREN'T A FUCKING DOG!" he bellows, standing up.

In the same way his laugh had filled the house, his voice *boomed*. I could feel everything around me shaking, and I trembled with a strange, clenched fear and crouched by the kitchen counter. My eyes are shut tight, and the kitchen and entertainment area blurred and vanished. Then, I was in the bathroom again at my neighbour's house, smelling like chlorine and crying as I sat on the cold tiles in my lime green swim trunks. I spat blood into the palm of my hand and saw the little tooth there. I could feel my father's eyes on me, and I saw his hand, a massive hairy paw come towards my face and collide with a resounding echo. Shame washed over me in a raging torrent, and heavy bricks of guilt hit me over and over, tossed in waves by an imaginary mob. Tears fell from my eyes as the moment became as sharp as a razor's edge.

"I'm sorry," I hear myself mumble.

I open my eyes, feeling extremely self-conscious as the man is crouching quite near to me. He rests his hand on my shoulder.

"It's Friday," he says. "The day before Saturday."

With my face stained with tears and my chest heaving as I sobbed openly, I nodded, not understanding why.

SATURDAY

I have never had such sweet sleep; populated with vivid dreams exploding in colour. I couldn't remember them all, but the first one was at a family outing. It was in the countryside somewhere, a place filled with tall trees with gnarled roots, a mixture of mint and almond in the air. I was kicking up dust with a slightly older cousin, who kept telling me about his plans to join the army. The day was slightly overcast, and everyone was scattered about. A long wooden table was covered with foil containers holding food, with curry stained Styrofoam plates stuffed into a small garbage bag hung on a nail at the table's edge, as half empty cups with Kool-Aid inside rolled around lazily if they were hit by a slight breeze. I walked through the event again, marveling at how lucid the dream was, stomping my feet on the ground, hearing the crunch of gravel on my small sneakers, feeling the blades of grass in my hand. Feeling the lightness and weightlessness of a little boy's body. One of my aunts, an old miserable woman, came over to me.

"There is something wrong with our family," she said. "We are always so angry and unrepentant. We need to change these things, change our lives."

The original memory had been frightening as she stood there, towering over me in a billowy floral dress, her face wrinkled and her eyes dark with thought. Something about my aunt had always scared me. She lived on that property alone, always hissing at cats that tried to sneak little bits of fish after she fried them, and threatening to hit me and my cousins with sticks for minor offences during boring summer days. That day, with the overcast sky as the backdrop behind her head, her voice had felt like an icy wind on my back.

"We need to change, do you hear me?" she had said.

This time, in my dream, I looked at her with a casual clarity, noticing the moles below her eyes, the slightest hint of grey hair showing under her cheap black wig and a slight bit of yellow crust in her left eye. I could see some curled hairs on her forearm, and a noticeable hole in the left sock she wore. Instead of the childish fear I had felt before, there was a pity that overwhelmed me, I could sense she was alone and angry, lost in a world of negative reactions. My father had always called her an old bitch. Possibly, other family members had also said the same thing. Now, I simply saw a woman in the later stages of life, with lines of regret etched into her face, her eyes tinted with the dark acceptance of past behaviour. Then, I walked into the house briefly and saw the picture of her and my uncle when they were young. She was slim, with flawless skin and beamed a smile of pure joy. He stood tall and resolute, showing a strong smile of white teeth. He had died ten years before. I left the house and walked outside, running into the dense enclave of trees behind the house. I ran and I ran, laughing as fat leaves slapped my face, and my nostrils burned with the pungent smell of underbrush. Then, I woke up.

Alert and relaxed, I take a moment to stroke the silk sheets I bought when I purchased the house, and look around the room. *It is big,* I realize. I stand up and walk to the window briefly, looking down at the garden, at the edge of a hill, overlooking the city. Most days I would look at this same vista, filled with dread about the upcoming day, the forays into social situations and establishments that come from going into the real world. I stand there calmly, staring at nothing and everything, feeling similar to the man from yesterday.

The man from yesterday!

I walk quickly downstairs. I hear a low humming noise that sounds like music. The kitchen is in a wild disarray of scattered pots and pans, with vegetables, broken slices of bread and jugs filled with juice everywhere. The humming is coming from the man, busy stirring something on the stove. *So strange,* I think. Whatever melody he is humming sounds so much like real music. He turns around as I approach.

"Hey man! Sleep well?" he asks.

Aware that I was standing in my boxers in front of a complete stranger, I nod sheepishly.

"Yes, I haven't slept that well in a while," I reply.

"Good, Good," he said, returning to his cooking.

In the distance the television is on. Images flash across the screen that I don't recognize. Voices in another language speak excitedly, and what appear to be Chinese characters flicker rapidly on screen. A man is running in a yellow tracksuit beside another man in the same outfit. They stop, panting heavily, and one of them says something to the other. The first man pauses and then says something in reply. Immediately the screen cuts to an audience of people laughing loudly, and the mysterious man in my kitchen starts laughing as well.

"You speak that language?" I ask.

"Language is life man," he replies. "Guys like you should really do more with these resources you have, but listen try this."

A pot is bubbling with a mysterious mixture of vegetables and rice together. He takes a spoon coated with a mysterious green powder, scoops some into a small plate and hands it to me. Whatever it is smells delicious. I take a fork from a nearby drawer and taste it. My mouth is quickly on fire with sensation. I can detect every hint of texture from each vegetable and get a sense of the variety of spices in the mysterious food. My brain tingles with pleasure. Barely able to contain myself, I say: "Wow, what is in this?"

The man laughs.

He replies, smiling, "You've just tasted the food of the gods."

Not wanting to appear desperate for a second helping, I relish the small morsel. The man laughs again at something on the television.

"You know, I don't even know your name," I say.

"You can call me Alan," he replies.

"Why were you in the garden yesterday?" I ask.

Alan smirks slightly, his eyes still on the television screen.

"I'm on my way home," he says. "Your lawn was a pit stop."

I rest my arms on the kitchen counter. "I don't get it. On your way home?"

"Remember I was looking up at the sky?"

"Yes," I reply.

"Sometimes in life, there are these moments, a mixture of symmetry and circumstance. You need to be in the right place at the right time to feel it. The synergy of life blends with the energy of everything around you, and you *feel it,* and then it goes poof! And it's gone forever. What happened on your lawn yesterday hasn't happened for about a hundred years."

A slight confusion crawls up my back, settling between my shoulders.

"What happened?"

"It's hard to explain really, but it has to do with the alignment of the clouds, the specific brightness of the sky, the wind factor, and the song of the earth."

"The earth can sing?" I ask.

"Like Barry White dude," he says with a slight chuckle.

"There is a symmetry of time and moment which creates a frequency that you can't hear. But this frequency fluctuates ever so slightly and it creates music, the most beautiful music you can imagine. If you heard it, tears would stream from your eyes and you'd be rolling in bliss."

"How can you hear this frequency?" I ask.

Alan's face falls flat, his eyes directed towards the floor. The TV, blaring seconds ago is a dull throb in the distance.

"I can hear it, because I'm what you would call an angel," Alan says.

"An angel!" I say with an incredulous laugh.

Despite the fact that I am in my boxers, in the kitchen with this strange fellow, my stomach clamps with a need to breathe as I laugh for a small eternity. I open my eyes to see Alan staring at me with abject seriousness. My need to laugh evaporates in a quick burst and I stand there transfixed, unable to move.

"There are events that take place in the quiet moments around us, and often we can't see it unless we really focus and let go of certain things in our brains. I felt one of these moments was about to happen and came on your lawn to experience it. In that moment, right here, I would never have felt that anywhere else, it was completely singular and unique and I was also able to share it with you."

"Share it with me?" I say.

"Yes, being aware of something doesn't mean there isn't value in company. Haven't you ever been out with friends of family and you didn't want to be there, but they seemed glad you were there? It's the same principle."

"Okay, I guess."

He laughs. "Just take it as a story from a traveler."

Alan was definitely odd, but there is something significant about his presence. Being close to him is like being beside a warm fire, or the feeling of eating candy for the first time as a child. Whatever energy he is exuding, I cannot quantify it. I also realize, for the first time in years I have not looked at any clocks. Could this guy really be an angel?

"You aren't gay, but you are worried about how comfortable you feel around me aren't you?" Alan asked.

I freeze.

"Somewhat."

"This feeling, we call it harmony. We angels emanate a low level pulse that creates calm and joy should we be around anyone."

"I don't believe it."

"You don't have to, but shortly before you were trying to kill yourself, you were drunk, depressed and mentally chaotic. How do you feel now?"

I stand there for a brief silence, completely unable to draw on the negative emotions that had guided my adult life for so long.

"I feel great," I say with a regretful tone.

"That's part of harmony at work. It can filter into your body and restore you from a bad state to a pure one."

"Can you read my thoughts? How did you know I wanted to kill myself?"

"I can't read your thoughts. Well not yet, not all of them anyways. I'm transitioning back to my original state."

"You mean going to heaven? Heaven is real?"

Alan chuckles at the TV, which is mysteriously back to its previous level of volume.

"Heaven is a human construct to process what we call *there*."

"There?"

"Yes, it is simply where I come from. I exist there in a different state of consciousness. Human emotions are like waves that we read. Voice waves are decoded into words, and emotional waves are decoded into intentions. Presently, as I'm shifting back into my higher state, even in human form, I'm able to decode feelings around me. But you are lucky that your front yard is the place that had the vibrational frequency I wanted to hear, or you'd be dead now."

"What? But you felt my 'waves' or whatever! You wouldn't have come to stop me? That doesn't sound like an angel to me!"

Not sure why, I am genuinely upset.

"Do you stop every fight you see on the road? You are a millionaire, but do you give every beggar you meet a dollar? In human terms you could say my need to witness a celestial event on your lawn was 'selfish' and the fact that you wanted to kill yourself was a 'coincidence'. Be thankful that my presence stopped you."

"I can't believe this is happening. You put drugs in my food or something. You aren't an angel! They don't exist!"

Alan smiles and looks down, at his shorts. "We are going out tonight, we need clothes, let's go to the mall."

As he smiles my anger and disbelief goes away. I go upstairs to my closet to get some clothes and feel disbelief turn into fear as I think that a random celestial entity is in my kitchen watching Chinese movies. I take a deep breath, put on some clothes and go downstairs.

THE MALL

On the way to the mall, Alan does not say much, mostly occupying himself by strumming his fingers along the passenger armrest. Cold air blasts from the air vents as usual. I am quite chilly, but Alan seems fine.

"So when do you need to leave town?" I ask.

"Sunday evening. I'm overdue for my trip home. I need to be at your place before I leave, if that's okay with you."

"It's fine," I reply, turning off the highway exit and into the sprawling, endless expanse of the mall's parking lot. We step out of the vehicle and walk towards the main building, a massive centralized behemoth with dozens of stores and restaurants.

Alan looks around constantly as we head into the main building, smiling at a drying puddle of discarded soda on the ground, children fighting over a handheld video game system and the blinking lights on a vending machine near the main entrance.

"Let's go to Armin," he says.

"Armin?"

"Yeah it's a good store."

I know the store. It is the most upscale store in the mall, with three hundred dollar t-shirts, eight hundred dollar shoes and customization services that cost an average person's monthly rent. I shop there often. Noise hits us as we stroll through a pair of large, transparent automatic doors; ears hit quickly by the sound of families and footsteps, shuffling bags and ringing cell phones. Normally I walk through the mall with my head slightly down, avoiding eye contact with most people until I enter Armin or another similar store, but today I walk with my head up and chest out. We make an odd pair; Alan in his khaki shorts and oversized grey shirt, and me in shiny slacks and a designer button up shirt. Each person we pass gives us a brief look and many, a lingering stare. Girls point and giggle. A young man with a loud shock of red hair walks up to me.

"Hey can I get a picture with you guys?"

"Uh sure," I respond.

The young kid holds up his phone and takes a picture of all three of us, expertly capturing our faces in the frame.

"Are you guys famous?" he asks.

Alan says nothing but laughs, replying soon afterward, "Probably so kid."

"Awesome!" the young man replies, darting back to a group of friends that look exactly like him, teenage-slim with skinny jeans and dyed hair.

This effect amplifies as we near Armin. Fingers point, a few more girls and guys want pictures and Alan happily services them all by doing thumbs ups, odd poses and goading me to do the same.

"So this is harmony," I say to him.

"Yes it is, but it isn't limited to me. Have you ever seen someone famous walk into a room and watch the energy shift? That person has harmony. But you don't even need to be famous, many people enter a place, a building, a room or a park and people start watching them, asking questions and wondering."

"Yeah but they aren't angels," I say with a smile.

"We can't all be perfect!" Alan retorts.

His face is glowing now, his skin clearer and smoother, the eyes more piercing and the voice more present. We walk into Armin's and I sniff deeply, relishing the scent of high-end leather and cologne. I stroke my fingers idly on clothing in the racks, loving the touch of silk, polyester blends and the stippled surface of some hot new designer jackets. I'd spent many hours in this store, browsing mostly. Armin's gave me something I didn't usually have in my day-to-day experience, vivid touch and colour. But my shopping had always been done quietly, as I tried avoiding the saleswomen, who were disarmingly attractive. One of them makes a beeline for us, a striking brunette with perfect eyes whose beauty seems wasted in this mall store.

"Afternoon gentlemen," she says. "Welcome to Armin's. I'm Jane and—ah! Mr. Wilson good to see you again! Would you like to put your purchases on your account?"

"Uh, yes," I reply nervously.

"Let me know if you need any assistance," Jane says, turning and walking towards another young woman who could be her doppelganger, folding shirts on a large white counter illuminated by soft strobe lights. I couldn't help but notice the firm bounce of her perfect derriere just before it disappeared behind another rack of clothing.

"Mr. Wilson?" Alan asks me with a smirk. "That isn't even your real name."

"Well I—"

"You are a funny guy," Alan said, leaning over a rack of lambskin jackets that cost twenty-five hundred dollars each. "Let's have some fun."

He hands one of the jackets to me.

"Ah, this isn't really my style," I say.

"What is style? Do you want to wear striped shirts everyday for the rest of your life? COME ON!"

In the background, Jane and her colleague talk to themselves, occasionally watching us. Another shopper, an older gentleman in slacks like mine wearing a similar shirt smiles at us. The next two hours are a blur of fast-paced jokes and me trying on tight pants and oversized shirts. Alan apparently, wants to buy everything, and both assistants are helping us, Jane and the other girl whose name is Maya. As we try on a variety of bomber jackets and leopard print pants, I find myself laughing hysterically. The numbness that I'd felt on entering the store was gone. Delicate nuances of certain feelings are now at the forefront of my mind. I can notice the subtle hints Jane throws at me as we try clothing on and the proximity with which she stands beside me. Mary throws endless sexual daggers at Alan without any consideration that she is at work.

"There is something about you two I can't put my finger on," Jane says, her hand a light, comfortable weight resting on my shoulder.

"Uh huh," I reply, trying to decide on oversized shirt she's recommended, that hangs slightly below my waist. "You sure this shirt doesn't look like a skirt?"

"Its all the rage right now Mr. Wilson, I'd pair it up with these boots and perhaps this jacket to take some of the attention off the length of the undershirt."

I put on both items quickly, shocked to see the person looking back at me in the mirror. It is a sharp young man with a slight smile plastered on his face, flanked by a dark beauty with smoky eyes. My heart races with anticipation, anticipation for *everything;* the feeling of becoming a new person, whatever grey area I was entering with Jane, and my clarity with which the future now holds. Despite the bland, functional lighting in the store, it feels rife with colour.

"Do you mind if I ask you what it is that you do exactly?" Jane says, her voice a whisper near my ear.

"I'm a software programmer," I reply, turning and facing her.

Standing this close to her was is a dream. The polished cheekbones, arched eyebrows and fully, pouty lips make my blood boil. Then I notice.

"Where's Alan?" I ask.

He is nowhere to be seen, but emerges moments later from a section of the store far from us with Maya, both of them with their faces slightly flushed.

Jane laughs to herself.

"I think I'm in love!" Alan says with a shout.

I stand there, disbelieving.

"We'll take everything," Alan says to Jane, dropping a heavy arm around my shoulder.

I can smell the fragrance of the other young woman wafting off him, something sweet and tender. She is enamored by him, and takes a few more seconds to stare in his direction before going to the cashier's area, fighting to not be distracted by whatever memories she had just created in a storeroom with Alan. If he has such an effect on me, I cannot fathom what it did for her, I think. As I pay for the clothes with my card, both girls pack all the items into several large and sturdy brown shopping bags with no discernible label.

"Jane and Maya will be accompanying us later," Alan says, his eyes hidden behind a pair of limited edition Gucci Aviators.

"Where are we going?" I ask.

"Wherever," he says with a smile. "But you aren't leaving the store like that."

Minutes later, I leave the store in a dark leather jacket, complimented by a black Zegna undershirt, and new Louboutin boots. Alan is hungry again, so we go to the food court. The previous effect we had was more powerful than before, especially as now our outfits are more striking. Alan is dressed like me, in a sleeveless leather jacket complimented by a black undershirt and a belt with a gaudy belt buckle that resembles a smiling face. He goes to order our meals and I sit at a table nearby, fingering a card in my pocket, one with Jane's number on it. Beside me, an invisible umpire shouts into my ears: *Anticipation! Excitement!*

I see Jane's eyes in my vision, dark and smoky, the lips speaking to me softly, her toned thighs straining against the fabric of her black work skirt.

"Hey man are you guys musicians?" comes a young girl's voice.

There are four of them by the table, barely past puberty, with bodies that are all straight lines and no curves.

"No we aren't," I say with a smile.

"Can we take a picture with you anyways? You guys seem really cool," the girl says sheepishly, resulting in a resounding giggle from her group.

"Why not."

Soon Alan returns with an enormous serving of Chinese food. The tray has servings of pineapple chicken, General Tso's, Lo Mein, fried rice, wonton soup, mushroom chicken, white rice and a box of steaming vegetables.

"LET'S EAT!" he shouts, bringing the food court, to a quiet, temporary silence. People stop in mid-walk; kids halt in the middle of eating and even the servers look up to see who had shouted.

"Funny, isn't a quiet moment in a large crowd what you call 'An angel passing through'?" Alan says, biting into a massive piece of pineapple chicken. As he does this, the lull of the food court returns. Then, he smiles again, saying "Eat up buddy, eat up."

PARTY

Jane is holding my hand as we exit the SUV and walk down the strip towards the club named SUTO. She leans against me occasionally as we make our steps together, her smell and presence mingling with mine, hair sweet with a hint of mint, her arms firm from a life of determined self-preservation. Maya is in a similar rhythm with Alan, as they chat in low tones to each other, walking a few feet in front of us. We are waved through the line by a giant bouncer and into the din of the club, which is filled with beautiful young people moving frantically under scattered strobe lights. Maya informs us that the club was originally going to be called "LOTUS", but the owner thought that would be such a common name he dropped the 'L' and turned it backwards. A man dressed in full black with the exception of a red vest ushers us into a VIP booth facing the dance floor, a curved seating area with a long stretch of black velvet couches. Things are a blur for a little while; broken conversations with Jane in between drinks about her aspirations to write non-fiction and see Machu Picchu while interacting with a wave of stunning women who keep drifting in and out of our booth. But my eyes are fixed on Jane, rooted in the memories of hours ago, when I was laughing at the store, really laughing for the first time in ages. Alan is making the rounds, dancing in the VIP booth and also on the dance floor, chatting to men and women at the bar and smiling in every direction. Our VIP space is getting somewhat congested and Alan waves at our server to keep the drinks coming. I take Jane away from it all for a moment, enjoying a song or two on the dance floor, her strong arms around my waist, my eyes closed, lips close to the nape of her neck. A hand touches me, and I see a sharply dressed young man behind me.

"Why is everybody going into VIP? Is your friend famous?"

I laugh and say, 'no', then resume getting lost in time with Jane. For a second I look up and see Alan in the midst of his VIP entourage standing up while everyone is sitting down. He is not smiling. Concern blankets me and I excuse myself from Jane, who accompanies Maya to the bathroom. As I approach our booth, I see Alan's face grow dark, his eyes tiny slits. He is not looking at me but behind me. I turn to see a man by the bar, almost hidden in the shadows, despite wearing a full white suit and matching fedora. He does not look in our direction, but at the ground, holding a glass in his hand. I re-enter the booth, shuffling past kissing couples and amped up young men drinking freely from our bottles of Grey Goose.

"Who is that?" I ask Alan.

For a beat, Alan does not respond, keeping his steely gaze forward.

"*We* don't talk to *them*," Alan says.

"Them?"

"Yes."

"Can you tell me more about that perso—"

Alan rests his hand firmly on my shoulder and immediately I become quiet. I can feel unnatural strength coursing through his fingers. He looks directly at me.

"No need."

His expression holds more than his words. There is a black void in his feeling towards the mysterious man by the bar, something from the depths of his reality he cannot express. Thinking about it, I feel the shadowy presence of the man amplifying in my mind, his odd stance by the bar, his unwillingness to look up, and the drink in his hand, full and untouched. I become worried and then frightened. If Alan is an angel, then who is the other fellow?

Alan snaps his fingers. I look up to see him smiling again, resonating his previous energy. "Let's get out of here."

We go to Karaoke with the ladies at a small Japanese restaurant nearby. Alan chats to the owner in fluent Japanese and has the staff bring us warm Sake. Maya and Jane do duets and one of the restaurant employees sings "Sweet Home Alabama" with all of us. Alan hands me the microphone. I frown, rubbing my temples.

"We aren't singing 'Don't Stop Believing' are we?"

Alan's face is masked with genuine shock.

"YOU READ MY MIND!"

We sing together, his arm around my shoulder, the girls on either side of us, all screaming till their voices are hoarse. So does most of the staff, since the restaurant is basically empty. We drink Sake and feel warm as the garish light from the screen watches us through the dark glasses of an actor riding on a Harley Davidson motorcycle in a video playing on repeat as the words of the song scroll downwards. We croon and laugh, singing Hip-hop hits and country ballads, Celine Dion throwbacks and the occasional Disney theme song. The Sake is kicking in, and Alan, impervious to the effects of the copious alcohol consumption, drives us all back to my place, his usual smile plastered on his face as the cool night air makes my eyelids flutter.

We are back at the house, and Jane is in my room, smiling at me as she slips off her dress, revealing her naked, toned body. She is a stark contrast to the blandness of the room, which I remind myself I need to update. The world around us disappears as she falls on me, her body warm and firm, her lips fast and everywhere. Blanketed by ecstasy the night goes on and on until we are both spent and covered in sweat, eyes closed, facing each other.

When I wake up, the house is deathly quiet. I walk past the upper room and see the door ajar. Clothes are strewn on the floor and under the huge sheets lies Maya, sleeping blissfully, alone. Down the stairs a moment later I enter the kitchen, which is immaculately clean, save a lone bottle of whiskey on the counter. I walk to the balcony. It is still night.

Alan is standing on the lawn almost exactly where he was when I first saw him. His shoes are off, but he is still wearing the stylish outfit from the Armin store. He stares up at the sky, unmoving. Something is different about him. His focus is completely on what lies above him and the sharp sense of myself I around him previously is not there. I dart down the stairs, exit the front door and step on the grass, the blades tickling my bare feet.

"Party animal, how are you?" Alan says, not turning around.

"I don't know," I reply.

"Of course you do."

I am assaulted by the pleasant images of the mall, shopping at Armin, the club and Karaoke time and Jane's exquisite physique. These memories are all charged by the peripheral presence of Alan, the catalyst for the flurry of pictures and attention we constantly received. I look at myself in the first part of this memory, in dull slacks and my buttoned up shirt, head held slightly low, and filled with fear. It is a far cry from how I stand now, back straight and resolute.

"Alan please! What can I do when you leave? I-I don't want to go back to how I was feeling!"

Beside myself, I feel tears running down my face, seeing the image of myself only a day before, on the balcony, ready to leave it all behind.

"It's okay *Mr. Wilson*," Alan says with a laugh in his voice. "Understand that there are rules that govern all movement and decision, things I cannot fully explain to you. But the beginning and ending of everything is always happening at the same time. Two sides of any situation exist with extreme clarity. It is for you to choose how you see it."

"I don't think I understand," I say, wiping my face.

"What do you truly want?" Alan asks, his back turned to me, his head looking upwards.

"I-I just want to be happy."

"Well look at where you are in just a day, with a beautiful woman in your bed, a renewed sense of self and you even have the courage to say to me what you've probably never told your psychiatrist. This is all because you did one thing."

"What is that?"

"You offered me a drink."

"Oh?"

"More than that you gave me an invitation. There was no need for you to invite me into your home, or even your life. That invitation is the other side of what could have happened. You could have cursed me and told me to leave your property, and I would have. But the *invitation* was an exercise that you alone choose to do."

"I see."

Alan raises his hands upwards, parallel with his shoulders.

"If you can invite a stranger into your house, you can invite happiness inside, every day, every hour, every minute, every second."

"How can I keep doing this?" I ask.

His presence is fading.

"Look at what you are wearing," Alan says to me, turning around.

I look down at my outfit, noticing I am wearing a dark grey shirt and loose fitting khaki pants. A smile finds me, and when I look up again, there is nothing in front of me except the cool pants and the leather jacket, folded neatly on the grass, the collar of the jacket pointed upwards directly to the endless array of white stars in the vast night sky.

Mr. Silver

I'm putting on my clothes in the mirror, noticing how shabby my hair is, but I don't mind, because my outfit with its tucked in sleeves, well knotted tie and designer pants still carry the weight of some dignity for me. Outside the sky yawns in a battle between truant night clouds and replacements ushered in by the burgeoning sunlight. I'm up a little earlier than usual, and walk to my bus stop with time to spare. A fog of silence covers the completely vacant street.

"Probably just me being early," I say to myself.

At my bus stop, I rest my work bag on the narrow bus bench. Slight movement to my left catches my eye. It is a man in a grey suit, standing at the corner of the building behind me.

"I have an offer for you," the man says, coming over and leaning his cane on the wall nearest to the bus bench.

I look at the man with his odd outfit. The suit he is wearing is grey, with a modicum of colour loitering in the fabric, waiting to burst out. He is not very tall, but possesses a strong air of authority. Nothing in him reflects anything other than who he is in his present form, wholly shaped and complete. I shuffle my feet and look into his eyes, caught by their stark, blistering intensity. As if sensing the exact moment of his impact upon me, he gives me a subtle smile with a slight opening of his lips.

"I have an offer for you," he repeats.

I look nervously on my watch and then back at him.

"What is the offer?" I ask, wondering why the time on my watch isn't changing.

A soulless smile creeps across his face, and he gestures with his hands, making a slight bow.

"I have the ability to take one of your most painful memories and make it go away," the man says to me, his smile now gone.

I laugh at this, but he continues speaking.

"There are terms to this agreement. Once you have decided on which memory you no longer want, you have one day to decide if you truly want that memory to go away. We take a journey through your various memories and remove the major one. Also, once the memory is gone, you can never get it back."

I snorted at this.

"There is a lot in life I'd like to forget," I say.

"Are you sure?" the man asks, standing quite still. "The building blocks of life are memories. Good or bad, they shape who we are through painful or joyous circumstances."

"I guess so," I reply to him, checking my watch again, which reads 7:02 AM.

Behind me, the street is completely empty and I strain my eyes to see if the bus is somewhere in the distance, wondering where the usual morning commuters are.

"But how can I even believe you?" I said.

He makes the lifeless smile once more and waves his hand over his head. I hear a *whoosh* and a bowler cap the same colour as his suit appears on his head, fitting perfectly.

"Interesting magic trick," I muse, slightly impressed.

The man gives a perfunctory nod.

"Most people see that and believe I can do what I said before," the man says.

I sit on the bus bench and cross my legs.

"Bah, anyone can pull a hat from somewhere, it is the oldest magic trick in the book."

"We both know the hat wasn't there," the man replies quietly. "If it wasn't there, you must ask, then *where* did it come from?

I breathe out, slightly bored, again wondering where the bus is. If I get to work late again, my boss would probably fire me this time. The man switches his cane from one hand to the other and looks me dead in the eye.

"You masturbated this morning in the shower thinking of Rinko Kikuchi, and the underwear you are wearing isn't the cleanest pair in your drawer."

My face contorts into a wrinkled mess of embarassment, then anger.

"Hey! Are you on of those perverts who spy on people?" I ask, now on my feet.

The man laughs in an odd cough.

"How could a pervert know that you have a thing *mentally* for Rinko Kikuchi?" he asks, staring at me.

I pause, thinking of how watching the movie *Babel* got me into Miss Kikuchi, and then think the man must be right and for a quick second feel fright, replaced by the part of me that is still worried about the bus arriving on time.

"Don't worry about the bus," the man says curtly.

What! Did he just...?

Now, I am beyond curious. The upcoming workday compared to this chance encounter is an empty, rotting garden.

"So now that you believe me, are you still interested in the offer?" the man says without a trace of impatience in his voice.

"What do you get out of this?" I ask.

"I get *enough*," the man replies in a light whisper. "But for this to work you must decide on the memory."

I think about the last several weeks of my life, with me wearing mostly the same suit or one that resembles it, 'fandangling' in the shower to images of Rinko Kikuchi, and going to work pressed under the large arm of my boss. Then I think of *her*.

"I'll do it," I tell the man.

"Good," he replies. "You have twenty-four hours to fully decide, and must meet me back here at the exact same time."

My watch still reads 7:02 AM.

"I'll be here," I say.

"Do not be a second late, or you will never see me again, and never have this chance again."

The man starts walking into an alleyway behind us.

"Wait, what's your name?"

"Call me Mr. Silver," he says.

He disappears around a corner, then a sudden blast of noise and air makes me jump. Behind me, amazingly, is the bus I'd been waiting for. The driver gestures at me impatiently and I also notice to the previously empty street is now teeming with life. I raise a hand to scratch my head, then I hear someone call to me.

I smile when I see the face of my longtime friend Shane. Always a bit precocious from childhood, being around him made me nervous to this day. I hadn't seen him in years, even though we worked just a few blocks away from each other. He hadn't aged a day, still tall and broad-shouldered, sporting a boyish head of ruffled hair, with a spotless face due to the fact that he'd never grown a beard. I however, like most men who shave had that light hint of grey spreading from under my neck to my earlobes. It was barely visible, but I hated it.

We sit in seats across the aisle from each other. He is typing on his phone with relaxed fingers, smirking every few seconds. I wonder who she is, his textual tryst; sitting at her office or in a bed stewing in the aftermath of their night before. She is of course, jaw droppingly attractive and buxom I figure. Shane must have sensed me watching him and I quickly close my eyes, pretending to be take a pre-work snooze. I count in my mind as the bus hisses with each stop. *One. Two. Three. Four.*

I open my eyes and look to my right, and Shane is gone.

Once i'm off the bus I cross the road and walk for two minutes to my work building. It is large, gray and completely unassuming from those around it, like a pack of nuns all the same height and weight. I'm a digital art assistant at a large magazine that specializes in young women's fashion. Most of my days are spent creating illustrations for the various articles about how to be sexy, how to avoid bad sex, and a plethora of articles about the various failings of the male species. The work isn't bad but repetitive, and by 9 A.M I'm twiddling my thumbs trying to come up with an image to support an article entitled "How To Tell Your Boyfriend You Can't Have an Orgasm". I give up for a moment and walk to the kitchen, past several cherubic staff who have the light energy only the super young have; where their evolution is based on what they percieve to be adulthood; drinking rapaciously, wearing too much makeup, growing a patchy beard or smoking cigarettes with the old heads in management who would trade ten years worth of salary for a full head of hair. I make a cup of coffee.

The strange man from earlier comes to mind. The trick with the cap was a bit unusual, I think. Perhaps it would be too much of a stretch to say *supernatural?* More coffee swirls its way down my esophagus and I think about *her.*

I'd met her in the rain. Not literally, but it was a rainy night, and I'd unceremoniously agreed to go Salsa dancing with some friends. We'd met at one of those posh Kingston hotels, gaudy with everything doused in gold paint, loads of shiny paraphernalia; man sized vases and a smattering of movie-villain style chairs in the lobby. She was sitting in a chair beside my friend Amy, who had invited me. She was in a tasteful summer dress, which didn't show much leg beyond the lower knee. Everything about her hit me with a quick punch; the striking luster of her eyes, the cheeks that morphed lightly into little hills when she smiled showing her clear rows of white teeth. Her sense of humor was a boon, as she played along while I mercilessly teased her about her *Mary Poppins* style dress. We joined the foray of the upscale Kingston bar, briefly squeezing past a mob of gyrating bodies of various ages to listen to contemporary pop music, then headed off to the open air of a party down the road at a place called The Spot to dance Salsa. I bought rum for the ladies and happily danced with her for the first time, tickling her neck with my lips, trying to sneak kisses. Soon, the sky growled indignantly. She grabbed my hand excitedly and pulled me onto the dance floor as the sky released a shower of rain upon us. Wet drops hit our skin like fat flies. Her shoes were gone, and her bare feet plopped audibly as we spun around blissfully out of time with the music, somewhat muffled by the torrential cacophony. Us in the rain took me elsewhere, out of the murk of fuzzy Kingston nights and the merry-go-round of similar parties and faces. I liked her smell, the delicate cool of her skin and the silky locks of hair that fell to her shoulders. I erupted in laughter later, reading a text from her that read: "I am THE fucking *Mary Poppins!*" Driving home that night, I saw nothing but her eyes and felt the lingering sensation of rain against our mutual faces. It wasn't just desire I had, but curiosity. From that point on we'd been together for three years, until she broke up with me. She was there, and then, she was gone.

My thoughts are interrupted by the shrill voice of my department manager, miss Kellerman, calling to me. Not to be described by any means as shy, today she is wearing a pink and black striped tube top, glittery leggings and earrings that looked like dried purple cauliflower. I walk to her and look at some page layouts for the magazine as we return to the belly of the office. When the day ends, my colleagues invite me for a drink, but today fatigue hugs me like a thirsty lush at an industry after party. The bus ride home is a blurry visage of mechanical hisses, honks and dull chatter. My mind is heavy with thoughts of *her*. I'm too tired to make dinner and fall asleep while watching a Gaspar Noé movie that totally confuses me.

****

He sits across from me in a resplendent red leather chair. His outfit is immaculate; a crisp, high end black suit still pungent with that fresh dry cleaning smell, complete with a matching dress shirt and tie. He sits with his elbows resting on either armrest of the chair, looking at me, but not speaking. We are in a dark room, vast and borderless. Above us, is some light source, but I see no bulb. We stare at each other for a while, saying nothing. Then he speaks.

"You're back," he says.

"Yes," I reply.

He sighs and takes a black handkerchief from his front breast pocket and dabs his forehead, even though he isn't sweating.

"Are you a fool?" the man asks.

"A fool? What do you mean?"

"This girl, this 'love', she obviously doesn't like you," he remarks.

I feel the sting of this statement like knives in my gut.

"Well," I start to say.

"Well nothing," he interjects. "Tell me, this 'love', does she respond to any of your messages in a timely fashion?"

I fidget in my chair, and then respond. "No."

"Also, this 'girl' seems to have a tendency to disappear in mid-conversation if she actually does respond to your messages yes?"

"Yes."

"And this 'person', does she make an effort to chat with you when she sees you in passing?"

"Well, not really. I mean she says hello, but—"

The man slams his hard on the leather armrest with a *pap!* Echoing through the vast space of wherever we are.

"I don't care about hellos! Does she ask you about your life, your work or how you feel in general? Does she ask you anything about *anything?"*

I pause again and look at the floor, for some reason my feet are bare.

"No," I respond with a sigh.

"Then my friend, a logical person would say the best thing to do is leave her alone. Has she happily chatted to persons near to you but ignored you?"

"Yes."

"Strangers as well?"

"Yes."

"So you are saying that she will happily have long conversations with people she doesn't *even know*, but completely ignore you?"

I grit my teeth. "Yes."

"And here you are, still thinking about her. What does that make you, a fool yes?"

"I'm not a fool."

"Well you are a goddamn fool to me," the man says.

I catch his eyes, dark brown and a little beady, steady and focused. I stand up and leave the room. Then, I wake up.

I've had this recurring dream ever since we broke up, when she was no longer everything like the sky and clouds, but just another person in the Kingston melee, drifting past me in a wave of perfunctory hellos and frigid hand shakes. Lying in the dark massages me with memory. Her beside me in the early morning, when even the Roosters were still in dreamland, and Kingston was blanketed with a light morning cool. It reminded me of some trips we took; the trivial, predictable kind that only couples have. She loved the mountains. Me, with skinny legs fit for brisk walks on flat pavement detested these excursions but a hug from her immediately quieted this annoyance. I remember the swath of undulating verdant terrain, reggae music blasting on the radio as her SUV grumbled valiantly uphill. She nearly fell off a rotting tree; her subsequent laughs so childlike I couldn't help but laugh also. For some reason I was never hungry around her and she'd marvel at the long stretches I went without eating. My friends would say she was sustaining me with her presence, that I was feeding on her energy and needed little else. She often blushed at my compliments, always immediately diverting to telling random anecdotes to stymie any further exploration of my true sentiments. On the wrong days this would infuriate me, as she stared at me blank and unresponsive when I tried to go further, past a wall I couldn't breach. Alas, she was always there. With me to pick up video games and objects from people I'd bought off the Internet, having dinner at late night cafés and in my apartment in my old boxers drinking tea, or watching movies on the couch. These memories I hated the most. I shop alone now, wandering wraithlike through indistinguishable supermarket aisles, searching for nothing and everything. The person I was then is quite alien to me, the kid who could hop into her little SUV and drive forever, as long as she was beside me. Those days she was everything and everywhere, like clouds in the sky and morning trips to the bathroom. I sigh, roll over, and go back to sleep.

****

I wake up without my usual grogginess and quickly get ready. My mind is clear and as I wash my face I see that it is heavily shrouded with palpable uncertainty. The walk to the bus stop is quick. Like yesterday, the entire street is empty, save Mr. Silver who stands in the same place in his grey, shimmering suit.

"Right on time," he says with a wry smile.

He gestures with his cane and I follow him down the alley he walked into yesterday. To our left is a regular industrial metal door, which opens on its own.

"More tricks," I say.

He doesn't respond but stands there, looking blankly at me. I sigh and walk inside. The door closes with an unusual *whoosh* and all is dark. Light returns and I'm in a narrow hallway, which resembles a hospital. Nothing about the place feels unusual until we reach the end of the hallway, which splits into a T exposing a giant corridor that stretches into infinity from left to right. An odd feeling pecks at my skin, a dense feeling of mortality. This place was somewhere *else*.

"Each window is like a root supporting the overall memory you want to lose," Mr. Silver says. "You need do nothing but walk past and look into each one."

Behind me, the hallway is gone and only the endless corridor remains. I step to the first windowpane and look in. Startled, I find myself standing in the National Arena, in Kingston. The air is thick with the scent of white rum and the murmuring voices of a captive audience watching a boxing match. Sweat flies as the boxers hit each other like sacks of meat. *Whooo!* The crowd shouts when one man pummels the other. *Whooo!* The crowd barks when one man falls to his knee, blood streaming down his face from a gash over his left eye. I am perched beside other photographers doing a part-time gig, taking in the grisly sensations of this human combat. Behind me the crowd is thick and mostly obscured by dim light. Somewhere in those onlookers she sits, legs crossed and eyes quiet, watching the match. At some point I say to her after getting a complimentary drink, 'Wow, what a great match!' to which I receive a light nod, and no verbal response. The sensation of feeling foolish after doing this threatens to overwhelm me, so I return to the stage and refocus on the battle in front of me; watching the men pound each other senseless. Thankfully the screaming of the crowd mutes whatever sad, unhealthy things my mind tries to tell me. The shouts, music and *click click click* of the camera shutters turn everything around me into a dull buzz. *Pap! Pap!* Sounds the noise of gloves hitting human flesh. *Ping!* Comes the noise of a sound effect for the start of another round. *Whooo!* The crowd screams again. The match ends and the crowd roar for the victor and leave the arena in a noisy swarm. I don't see her leave. My phone buzzes with a text from her.

Sorry we didn't chat! See you soon :)

This I knew was a lie. In this memory I hadn't seen her in months. Then I hear *Clap!* And I'm back in the ethereal corridor, reeling with confusion.

That was so real!

I try and take a breath and notice that I'm in already front of the next window then—

I'm lying on my bed. Her hair spills onto my thighs and she pulls off my shorts. The day outside is quiet, save the occasional bark of a neighborhood dog. This doesn't feel like a sexual moment, it feels like a time for gardening or a midday nap, but she is pulling off my pants and her hair is on my legs, swishing and swaying. My entire body responds to this feeling of exclusivity; our youth and our peace, the fun and time that comes with exploring random moments. She holds my erectness in her hand for some time, admiring it, running her fingers up and down its length while kissing my thighs. Her eyes sparkle with intention and slowly she opens her mouth and—

The day is gone, and it is nighttime. Embarrassed, I feel myself fully erect, again in the otherworldly place with the man in the suit.

"What? What happened?" I ask, spinning around in the memory of that day, thinking of her silky hair and the mischievous eyes.

"Nothing happened," the man replies, his voice unchanging. "As I said before, we will be shifting through the memories. Some will be long, others short."

A part of me is still spinning with the blissful feeling of that dry summer day, slowly dissipating into nothingness. Now, we are in the same room but at a different time, lying together and speaking but and I cannot hear what we are saying to each other. But I can clearly see tension in her body. She stands up, pointing a finger angrily at me. I stand up as well, shouting and gesturing. The volume of our speech begins to pickup at a low speed. Like turning on a radio.

Dfdkflsjfds.fdsfklg;ajkg You.df.dsfl.. SAID...

"What do you mean you want to see someone else? After you spent the day with me!"

I can feel the blood in my veins like a clock ticking in my pocket. The feeling is so strong I cannot believe this is a memory. My mind briefly sparks with the image of a sunset and us holding hands, but it is foggy. *Where was it? Where did we go?* It was getting hard to remember now.

Clap!

The dress is high end, close fitting and vibrant with a dull shimmer from the lamplight. Her thighs shine as well, nice and toned, teasing me with the potential of what lay beyond, but she is a tad drunk, her eyes glassy and her face devoid of a smile. But I am mostly observing myself, more drunk than she is.

"I, I don't remember this," I say to Mr. Silver, turning around.

Nothing is behind me except unending black and a wailing, ice-cold wind. I turn back around. I see myself fixing another drink.

"You don't even know me," she says, standing up.

"Of course I know you," I say with a slur. "Every inch of that body."

"My mind, you idiot!" she screams.

She recites a highly crafted epistle of profanity at me. I let out an inebriated series of weird chuckles and saunter awkwardly towards the bedroom, seeking pillows and their promise of comfort. *This isn't right*, I think. I have no memory of this! My head feels heavy and I see things in flashes; my anger at her before she left, screaming at her for being distant, then her hands clutching my chest asking me not to leave before quickly changing her mind, me seeing the world in red and feeling a knot so tight in my stomach I barely ate for days afterwards.

"Funny how we don't always remember the most powerful moments," came the voice of Mr. Silver, to my left.

I pause. Mr. Silver's body is now double its density. He stands slightly taller, fitting poorly in the shimmering suit, which is tearing at the seams, his eyes are white and he licks his lips lasciviously. His musculature is unusual, with extreme distortions in the ratio of his chest to his legs, and his hands, which are now elongated and feral in appearance. With each scream or curse I hear my ex-girlfriend make behind me, I see his body ripple and pulse, the veins bulge, the muscles twitch and distort. He starts laughing as I realize what is happening. Then, he's gone and I'm back in the room.

She stands beside me, passed out on the bed.

"I wish you would understand," she says.

All falls silent. Then a slight noise comes from within the apartment. Light footsteps echo from the foyer and rise to full volume as a figure emerges from the shadows. Shane.

Shane? What the hell was he doing there? I feel embers of rage spark inside me. His eyes are slick with liquor, and a fiendish grin is on his lips. In this *other* place I'm able to see everything at once; my face smothered in a pillow while I lay in a fetal position on the bed, unconscious, and *Her*, considerably more sober than I, standing beside the bed. She looks at me for a moment before stepping into the living room.

"Is he asleep?" Shane asks.

Her finger on his lips stops his words.

"He never wakes up when he's this drunk."

Then she starts taking off his pants.

Wet panic smothers me as all is unveiled. I turn around, peering into the void, but see no one. No sign of Mr. Silver, planet Earth or anything I know. Closing my eyes doesn't help as I hear them romp from kitchen to couch all while I lay unconscious in the bedroom. Once finished, she slips the dress back on and Shane, not having removed anything but his trousers, casually zips up and leaves. His wink at her lets me know they've done this before. My thoughts screech like startled birds as I envision all the times Shane and *Her* tried to get me drunk. It was our silly group game I thought, but the joke was on me! I reach forward angrily, to clutch *Her* but everything in my vision shrinks in quick pulses, like a can being crushed in a vacuum. My fingertips are fat with pressure and I feel hot and brittle like an over boiled egg.

"You knew this was an odd choice," came the light timber of Mr. Silver.

I spin around, squinting in the blackness, but see no one. His voice is loud and everywhere like a projection system in a movie theater.

"Ladies and gentlemen, please find your seats, the movie is about to begin," Mr. Silver says with a chuckle.

The corridor upends and becomes a chasm I fall into, screaming. Colors around me shift rapidly between brilliant white, red, amber and green. Now I lie somewhere in dim light. A massive silhouette emerges from the shadows. Mr. Silver towers above me, inhumanly bulky, the suit torn off his body, standing naked in a sea of veins and odd proportions. His arms are so long they go past his knees, with a dot of a wrinkled phallus barely visible in a giant thicket of gnarled pubic hair attached to tree trunk thighs and oblong feet. I feel nothing but abject horror.

"I'm glad you agreed my proposal," he says in a voice several octaves deeper than the one I was accustomed to. "This is my ambrosia."

My mouth opens to speak but I am elsewhere, in a house with an odd familiarity. Red light streaks through large windows above me and fall on black and white tile. All is quiet, and nothing save a large, grizzled white dog lying in front of me. A musty odor rings throughout the house like church bells. A foggy window nearby reveals a barely illuminated, jagged and completely foreign horizon. I tremble, knowing that in this place significant time has passed. But how much? I sense I am also in this house presently, somewhere, in one of its dark rooms, sitting alone. I hear myself counting. *Counting what?* Fear lances my chest but I am unable to speak.

"This is where memory ends," says Mr. Silver, his dark voice booming throughout the house.

The dog in front of me begins twitching in a furor of spasms, spinning around like a top before mewling at a shrieking pitch that threatens to burst my eardrums. I clamp my ears shut with my hands, screaming also. Then all was red, and then all was nothing.

****

I hear a voice, dull but insistent. Brilliant light hits my eyes as I squint in the unmistakable luster of an early morning.

"Would you like a tissue young man?" comes the mild voice of an older woman.

"I'm sorry, why do you think I need a tissue?" I say to the woman.

She smiles in a calm sea of wrinkles. "Because you were crying son."

Sure enough, the light remains of tears were on my face, but for what reason, I had no idea. Dabbing my face with her tissue, I hear the bus arrive. I open my wallet to get my bus card. *That's odd,* I say, noticing a picture of young woman right above my license. She is very attractive, with long silky hair, striking eyes and a calm demeanor. 'Melissa' is written at the bottom of the picture. *Must be some kind of mix up,* I say to myself. I take the picture out of my wallet and throw it away. The bus roars to a start and I head to work, already dreading the day ahead.

Gaijin Girl

She always wore yellow shoes and no one knew why. If outside were a milky blizzard with frigid winds screaming at the world, she'd still be wearing the shoes. It's hard to ignore Yuka. When she sweeps into the bar, she is all smiles and sweet breath, hot hair and light makeup. Her love for foreigners she says is from old television programs she watched in hotels around the world.

Dashing, is a good word to describe her. In fact, she is always talking about her favourite words. One of her all time favourites is the word "duplicate" and no one really knows why. Once, she entertained a group of tall Eastern-European businessmen for an hour with stories loosely based on the word duplicate. For some reason her linguistic yarn seemed interesting. It wasn't what she said it was who she was, *genki* in that Japanese way, uncharacteristically tall and beautiful.

She shopped at the Gap and Hilfiger, wore Ralph Lauren cardigans and subscribed to GQ magazine. "Guys really like it," she tells people. If you don`t know Yuka, if you are ever in Tuddy's pub near Haruki Street and you hear a laugh that sounds like a spiraling crash of Christmas bells falling to the floor, then you'll know Yuka is nearby.

When you see her, the scene is always the same. In a group of large, white foreign men, she will be in the middle, the dim bar light bouncing off her flawless face and accentuating her hair. Her cheeks will be slightly rosy from drinking, but so far, no one can tell the difference between her drunken state and her sober one. She is in many ways, an enigma. After the laughter dies down and people are heavy with the desire for sleep or sex, you'll see her leave, giving the bartenders a kiss on the cheek, then take the hand of her prize for the night, and walk out the door.

The silhouette replays in my mind like a renaissance painting. If it existed we would see a dark street with cobbled stones and quiet buildings; the black shapes of a large man holding the hand of a statuesque, slim woman. In this picture the obvious highlight, almost obscured by all the shadows, are the yellow shoes, which even in the darkness shout from the canvas, raising question marks. Who is she? The casual observer would ask, if this were in an art gallery museum. Why the yellow shoes?

Many people called her a man-eater, a slut, a party girl. She was one of the girls the drunken foreign guy with the annoying personality could go home with on a Friday night. This reputation however, didn't stain her. New men in town heard about her; the girl with the yellow heels and many tried to seek her out. But like a ghost, she disappeared and reappeared at will, sometimes with a gaggle of girls with *chairo* hair and too much makeup, other times with a new foreigner from a nearby town or big city.

Sometimes she wore regular shoes; silvery pumps with glitter on the laces, or schoolgirl shoes with funky tassels. Occasionally she would even look plain, if such a thing were possible. Even in a thin Rolling Stones band t-shirt and jeans she was striking. Her eyes were unusually large and bright, and her smile hit you like a train. Sometimes you might run into her at a café or local store, as she shops for the latest American clothing, or gets her favourite CDs at the electronics store. If she sees you and says hello, it is like being greeted by someone who is thinking about you all the time, everyday. Her face will light up and her smile will poke you in the ribs. She'll ask you what you are doing, and whatever it is, mundane as it might be, you will feel great that she asked. A chill will run up your spine and an unusual tickle of appreciation will hit you. Maybe this is why she elevates past the level of man-eater.

There are some who talk about her in hushed tones at bars, after having a few drinks. They talk about her threesomes; the orgies with foreign men in posh hotel rooms while girls sitting topless with jeans on record everything with video cameras. You might hear, if you are standing close, about the time she gave a person head in a car outside a local park, or how a misguided guy fell in love with her and fought with a friend over her, while she went home with someone else. There is talk of the crazy parties, her alcoholism and how she lives in her own world to such an extent, its like no one else exists.

To say she is wealthy is an understatement. The bags and accessories change like paper towels on a busy Saturday at a truck stop. The brands are top-notch: Gucci, LouisVuitton, Hermes and Dolce & Gabbana. Someone said she also own a Birkin bag, which costs about six years of mid-level salary. Still, she doesn't come off condescending, and is happy to buy you a drink. I still haven't bought her one yet.

Her apartment is rumoured to be a lush den of opulent debauchery, with a phalanx of massive flat screen TVs, rugs made from wild animals, elegant marble floors and high end sex toys encased in glass displays. Some say she made sure not to have Tatami mats or too many Japanese things in there. I hear inside is an architect's ode to western interior design. Apparently each room has sultan mattresses, American bought linen sheets, an Andy Warhol painting and those little lights that you tap to make them turn on in the dark. There are lava lamps, pictures of U.S Celebrities and models, and a George Foreman grill. I heard she even flew in a Black & Decker coffee maker from the States to make sure she was making "real American coffee". Her American accent is flawless, and when you speak to her initially, you might think she's a citizen of the states. After a few drinks the Japanese side of her starts to slip out bit by bit, and she'll slur the L's and the R's like most of the Japanese do, then you'll say, "I thought you were American," and she'll reply with a resounding *Thank you!*

They say she started learning English as a little girl; sitting in her room wrapped in Winnie the Pooh blankets watching reruns of Beverly Hills 90210. Most likely she went to an intense language school, or learned on her travels. Apparently, she's been to thirty countries and lived in four, but I can't be sure. She went to college in the states I hear, and fell in love with a heartthrob who eventually became a professional athlete. No one knows the name of this person or what sport he plays. It is impossible to think someone like Yuka could even be in love. Her face is ever the mask of emotional contentment, never shifting, never changing. She seems born to be loved, and gaining access to her space is more like a privilege that something one can consciously achieve.

She is tall, with long legs, silky hair that falls to the middle of her back and pseudo-European features. Naturally you will think she's Japanese (and she is), but there is something extra in her looks, an outcropping of the west in delicate touches. One can see the straight bridge of her nose, the modified slant of her eyes and her fuller than average lips. If a plastic surgeon did some work on her, then she is his *magnum opus*. I heard someone ask her if she was a model once, and she just laughed, filling the room with bells, and continued sipping on her drink. Sometimes I wonder if her overwhelming desire to love all things west is infused with her DNA, a tinkering experiment.

No one really knows what she does, or why she occasionally reappears in this small Japanese town. Apart from a few theatres, low-level clubs and a large statue of a fish in the town square at its main attraction, it's not the place for a world-roaming, socially savvy butterfly like her. Some people think its because it's her original home, and despite the men, the traveling and the money, it's who she is. A little girl who once romped on Tatami mats and ate noodles for snacks in hot Japanese summers.

There are stretches of time when she disappears, and Yuka is on the lips of all in town. Where is she? What is she doing? Did she leave Japan? The foreign men eager to touch her perfect breasts or run their hands through her hair also wonder where she is, the girl with the yellow shoes. Once I heard she met a man in Tokyo, a Danish fellow who's family were the major shareholders in a global electronics corporation. This man, I heard, was tall, blonde and blue-eyed, handsome and muscular, intelligent and wealthy—all things Yuka likes, but he was not American, so his perfection was smeared, like toothpaste on a diamond. The story says after a whirlwind affair of country hopping, Yacht parties and his proposal to her outside a nightclub in Shibuya, she said no, and disappeared soon after with her latest flame, an American surfer staying at a hostel in Asakusa.

The last time I saw her, she was standing outside the local mall, looking at a display window. On the front of the store, were three heavily muscled models in briefs with intense expressions. She laughed as I said hello. "You caught me fantasizing!" she squealed. I laughed along with her. Now it is a cold day near the end of the year, and dark leaves fly through the air against their will. Heavy wind makes old boards creak and groan, and all is still in the quietness of the night. Sometimes, on a cloudy day or a quiet night I'll walk with my coat wrapped tightly around me, and in the distance I'll see a couple walking hand in hand, and I'll smile, wondering why the lady wasn't wearing yellow shoes.

An Elephant in Kingston

People tell me that they saw an elephant in Kingston and I could not believe them. These were members of my family, friends, co-workers and people at my workplace. As my fingers shuffled through the ledgers I'd touch each day the numbers didn't seem to add up. Outside, the day bright and clear with spots of white, wispy clouds became tinted with the yellow of dismay and confusion. I'm a pretty average guy. I listen to a little radio, read novels every now and then, and when I get home to my wife, I rarely do anything other than missionary if she feels frisky. When I heard this story, I saw my right index finger trembling, as if it was signaling something to me. What exactly, I couldn't put my finger on, so to speak. Despite the time being only eleven-thirty in the morning, I excused myself briefly from the office. I'd already been working there ten years, and my 'tenure', as it were, allowed me some freedom to make excursions without notifying any staff of my whereabouts. It was a Wednesday, and Wednesdays were never quite busy. The company sold mostly stationery supplies and I wasn't under high pressure to figure out the marginal cost of new boxes of pencils. So I got up from my desk, nodded at a young man who had recently started working at the office, and headed outside. The man didn't nod in reply.

The sun felt nice on my face. I walked down a meager flight of steps in front of the office building, turned right and walked a block away to a stall at the corner of the road which faced a traffic light. Noise and heat hugged me warmly. Despite the time, the vendor from whom I often buy snacks smiled at me as if it was lunchtime. He was a small man, wiry with sinewy arms and a mysterious scar along his left cheek. His eyes were his greatest asset; bright and cheerful, not too large, not too small.

"Morning," I said cheerily. "You heard about this Elephant business?"

"Yes mi bredrin," he replied. "My friend saw the Elephant walkin' through Half-Way-Tree with a hat on."

"The elephant was wearing a hat?"

"Yeah man! Plenty people follow the elephant until it walk 'round a corner and dissappear."

"An elephant in the middle of *Half-Way-Tree* just dissappeared?"

"Yeah, it was strange," the man said. "One man say the elephant even talk."

Impossible! I said to myself.

"Well me wasn't there, but people say it, so I believe it," the man said, chuckling through a smile of missing teeth.

I didn't want to, but I had to believe him, because there were press reports about the elephant's appearance. Mysteriously, despite the plethora of individuals at the scene when the animal appeared, there were no photos of the animal to be found. This more than anything was an even bigger mystery to me.

"Nobody took photos?" I asked, reaching over a sea of lollipops and assorted snacks for a pack of Banana chips.

"Not one," the man said, quickly sliding my fifty dollar bill into his waist pocket.

As I munched on the chips I pondered this information. Why would no one take photos? One article I'd seen with the title "ELEPHANT'S GHOST?" in a small tabloid publication had a photo of the creature, but it looked extremely doctored, most likely a sales ploy. I left the vendor's stall, walking away from the office in no particular direction, my mind raging with images. My humdrum existence didn't seem so banal anymore. Around me, the streets in the financial district were hot and sparsely filled with the bodies of office workers moving to the symphony of vehicular traffic. I glanced at my watch and looked at the time. I was already gone for twenty minutes and needed to get back to the office. Despite my 'tenure', it wasn't my name printed on the front of the office building. So I returned to my office, welcoming the cool air that gently massaged my face. For the second time I nodded at the young man, who, for the second time did not nod back at me. I traipsed through the modest office space and sat back down by my desk. My computer screensaver was a bizarre menagerie of photos that someone had programmed into the device long ago that I never bothered to change. I tapped a key and the screen went black briefly, before showing the garish white glow of my office accounting software. I sighed and picked up some fresh sheets of paper to take to the office printer. The fresh paper immediately (and cleanly) sliced the tip of my left index finger, dripping little dots of blood onto the sheet. Standing by the office printer sucking my finger, I winced at the mild pain from the papercut. I thought again about the Elephant. I saw images of its bulk, thick hide, aging tusks and long snout with the bustle of Half-Way-Tree in the background; that chaotic rabble of policemen, hustlers, itinerant workers and goers about. As I watched the machine spew sheets of paper filled with numbers I really didn't care about, I wondered about my life. Why wasn't I out there? In the know? The most I was afforded was a glimpse at the outside world through a dusty window covered in more grill than window pane. I looked on the clock, it was only twelve p.m now, with several hours left in the day.

* * * *

On the way home, I turned on the radio, because evening traffic in New Kingston is a complete nightmare. In pretty much any direction, the bottleneck extends in a slowly moving caterpillar of a line for at least two miles, which equates to no less than forty-five minutes to an hour to exit the meager confines of the financial district. I was absentmindedly listening to the radio, when some words caught my ear:

There has been no further update on the mysterious sighting of an Elephant which was seen in Half-Way-Tree only days ago. Witnesses say the Elephant, which purportedly wore a pink hat and seemingly materialized into thin air, vanished soon afterward, after taking the left turn at the intersection of Half-Way-Tree-Road and Hagley Park road. Should any further news come to light about the animal, also known as a 'Pachyderm', we will immediately let our viewers know.

The last part of the news report missed me, because I was laughing. Harder than I had laughed in years. My body shook with the force of this laughter as it rose in a crescendo throughout my entire system. The force of this laughing became a convulsion, so much so that I had to pull briefly to the side of the road, my abdominals hurting with pain and my chest heaving for air. This of course, was to the amusement of several pedestrians walking by. The image of the large animal, tottering around the corner as if it knew where it was going hit me with another wave of convulsions. It was ten minutes before I turned my indicator back on, and drifted back into the traffic snaking into the horizon.

At home, I walked with extra pep as I entered the house. My wife, as usual, was watching her six-thirty p.m soap opera, sitting in a conservative skirt with the television remote resting on the armrest beside her. Despite this scene, which I saw every day except weekends, seeing her sit there was like seeing her the night I'd met her, in the dark confines of a bar playing soft reggae music; the lights above us reflecting off her smooth dark skin. I stormed over to her and grabbed her hand.

"Honey?" she asked, smiling meekly.

I didn't respond as my blood was boiling. We went immediately to the bedroom, where, after several excursions (and a few new tricks) we finally lay back, spent and tinged in sweat, our mutual chests heaving in the quietness of our bedroom.

"My goodness, what got into you today?" my wife replied, running her left hand across my navel, eventually resting it on the soft bed of hairs between my chest.

I laughed and hugged her, relishing her company and the softness of her body beside me. My loins stirred once more, and again, I was on her, lost in the sensations. Afterward, as she was in the bathroom taking a shower, I tried to process my current state. I felt renewed and charged up, and for only one reason: this Elephant business. I'd laughed for the first time in years, and the infrequent engagements me and the missus had multiplied tenfold in one night. It was decided, I had to find the Elephant. So the next day, I called into work sick.

Of course, it was Fredrick, my boss, who answered. Though I forcibly croaked through a napkin, sounding more like a silly cartoon than a sick version of myself, Fredrick had no issues with me taking the day off, even suggesting I take two if I need it. A part of me smiled inwardly, I guess I did have 'tenure'.

In the morning I headed out early as usual, opting for a casual pair of slacks and a short-sleeved shirt instead of office clothes. On a regular work day, I'd normally drive past a few avenues and down Constant Spring road towards Half-Way-Tree, where my office was based in a plaza across one of the huge buildings a telecommuncations company owned. But this time I went straight through the intersection past the plaza, headed through Crossroads then drove past the National Heroes circle. At this time of morning, before the major traffic started, a light cool drifted upwards from the street. It gave the illusion of a frigid, empty city devoid of people with nothing but traffic lights to guide whoever decided to traverse its depths. But there were a few signs of life; men wearing red and orange vests sweeping the streets, a vendor or two opening up shop and those folks that are always earlier than everyone else. I drove around for some time, passing by the Edna Manely school of art, looped up Mountain View avenue and drove near another university, the University of Technology or UTECH, where I walked around for a little while. Then I left UTECH, drove down Mona Road, and did another drive through and walk at the Univeristy of the West Indies, or UWI. Why was I doing this? Well, the only place I think an Elephant could conceivably hide in Kingston that had enough space was either on the University campuses or in Hope Gardens, which coincidentally had the zoo was as well. I didn't spot the Elephant on any of these premises and I almost had another fit of laughter imagining the chaos an Elephant in a pink hat would cause on a college campus. So I drove back through the back gate of UWI, and down Old Hope Road, towards Hope Gardens.

It was beautiful, seeing the vista before me at this time of day. In fact, I had no real memory of the last time I was here. The memory wasn't strong, but in it, I could smell food and feel the presence of friends or family, but I wasn't sure whom specifically. The Gardens were teeming with plant life carefully curated on a two hundred acre property. There were a few enclosed spaces—a narrow walkway here and there—and some areas with hedges grown high, but I knew the Elephant wasn't here. This was because you could see most of the property wherever you went. I scanned the horizon and saw nothing but grass and ancient trees. A pink-hatted, lumbering Elephant would have stuck out like a naked man screaming at me to get his attention in the middle of an empty soccer field. I walked slowly back to the car, which was parked some distance away. At the very least I thought, I could enjoy some of the free day, and I took a moment to sit on a bench. I closed my eyes and felt the air and the atmosphere coalesce into a cool, welcoming blanket. My lips curled into a smile thinking about the rousing time I had with the missus the previous night. Soon I opened my eyes, chuckling in embarassment at the obvious erection I had in my pants. Then, it came to me.

Recently in preparation for a major sporting event, the National Arena had been closed for renovations. These renovations were almost complete (as my trusty radio broadcast had recently informed me). The Arena space was huge and could easily hide an Elephant. I tried to calculate how that would work exactly, how to measure an Elephant relative to the square feet in the National Arena, but I gave up. I did accounts and ledgers, not volumetric calculations or titration. My watch said the time was now two p.m, which meant that I could search for the Elephant for at least two more hours before I could safely beat the evening traffic. I drove back down Old Hope Road and turned back onto Mountain View avenue, which was adjacent to the National Stadium. The massive structures of the Stadium and National Arena loomed in my vision like wraiths. As my car puttered towards the gate, I realized I had no idea how I was even going to get inside. As a security guard began to approach the gate of the stadium, my heart began beating faster. I didn't know what to sa—

"Afternoon sar," the man said. "Your business?"

I put on my cheeriest, business-man accent.

"Yes, just here to confirm a few things on site with the renovation. The boss sent me down," I said, staring directly at the young man.

The guard, obviously underpaid and bored, mulled over this information briefly.

"The boss sent you? Mr. Watson?" he asked.

"That's right young man, would you like to call him?" I said, a bead of sweat forming on my brow.

"No sar, that's okay, drive in this way and park over there," he said with two gestures of his hands.

As I drove into the National Arena I felt that similar rush I'd felt the night before with my wife. I hadn't been this adventurous or excited in years. Apparently, I had a serious deficit in both adventurism and laugh time. These were things I mentally noted that I needed to change. Once I parked the car under an adequately shady spot, I started walking towards the arena with my shoulders fanned out and my gait full of purpose, just in case the guard was still watching me. There wasn't anyone near the entrance, which still had a few signs of renovation; flecks of fresh paint on the entrance wall, a forgotten box of tools and a few planks of wood near the main entrance. As I stepped in, everything became unusually dark. Normally, when I walked into the National arena, I could see from where I was to the very end of the arena hall, but now I felt as if I'd stepped into a huge, black room. Even weirder was the time. It was only two-fifteen with loads of sunlight outside. My instincts began flaring up as I took a few steps further, now almost enveloped by this darkness. Then a thick, burning smell filled my nostrils quickly. The smell of animal dung.

I felt a sudden, impactful excitement. I had smelled dung! The Elephant must be here! Still, I winced at the smell, then squinted at something near my feet, an object I had almost stepped on. It was a long oblong box, completely black and spotlessly shiny. In fact, as my eyes adjusted to the darkness I could see that a series of these boxes were at various positions all around the massive open space. The alignment of these objects made me think of something I'd seen as a child in a class about magnets and the patterns they make around things like iron filaments. My skin crawled. A part of me felt extremely far removed from my office, Half-Way-Tree and even Jamaica itself. The darkness around me was a thick fog. It was also deathly quiet. If the Elephant *was* here, he had the movements of the Chesire cat, or he was sleeping. Despite my excitement at figuring out where he or she was, the faintest tingle of fear crawled up my back. I walked forward slowly amidst the black oblong boxes, which increased in number every few feet leading towards the back of the central area. There must have been hundreds of them, in the pattern I'd observed, with none stacked one on top of the other. Then I heard it, a low humming noise coming from one of the boxes. Upon closer inspection, I could see that it wasn't paint on the boxes, but some scaly, shimmering metal I couldn't identify. The sound it made was cool and hypnotic. I moved my hand towards the box, wanting to feel its rhythm.

"I wouldn't do that if I were you," a deep voice said from behind me.

I froze in place and slowly turned around. There, about twenty feet away was the Elephant. My hand still outstretched, fingers inches away from the box, I stood in place, my mouth agape. Everything about the Elphant seemed normal by appearance, but I knew it was different. Firstly it was the posture of the animal. On its massive haunches it stood on two legs like a man, with a pair of long black strips wrapped around the base of each leg. I also noticed the 'hat' it wore, which was actually a sort of dark coloured box that rested atop its head. It held something resembling a black wand in its trunk. The eyes were striking. Elephantine, but intelligent. It's forelegs were folded in a discerning, parental way, like arms.

"Each box holds several thousand kilowatts of energy, should you touch it, you would fry like the most burnt jerk chicken in human history," the animal said.

Now I felt afraid. I mean, this was an *Elephant* speaking to me!

"Kilowatts?" I stuttered.

"Yes, it's a unit of measurement you humans use to measure electricity," the Elephant replied matter of factly, forelegs still folded.

"I-I know that," I replied somewhat defensively, now standing with my arms also folded.

The elephant tilted its head down slightly, as if peering at me through a pair of horn-rimmed glasses.

"I don't have lots of time to explain the math to you, but you are standing in an array that creates a portal between dimensions. It requires tremendous power to do such things, as you can imagine."

I nodded as the creature spoke at length about complex physics, all of which went completely over my head.

"Forgive me," the elephant said. "You must be wondering why I'm here."

"Y-Yes," I replied.

The elephant sighed in a long, loud hiss of air and began walking towards me. The footsteps made no noise as it approached.

"Stabilization rigs on my legs allow me to move like this," the Elephant said to me as if it were a normal thing. It paused and looked at me again while leaning over one of the long oblong boxes.

"I'm not really an elephant you see," the creature said with a chuckle. "Where I'm from, I am how can I put this, on a different *frequency* so when I travel between dimensions I need a different body. For some reason I got an Elephant's body instead of a young human's body. I'm gonna have a grand time cursing the people in HR at the interdimensional transport company when I get back."

Behind the Elephant, the long stretch of the National Arena seemed endless and darker than before. Another shudder of cold feeling iced my veins. Something told me I wasn't in the National Arena anymore.

"So yes, I came here and to my surprise found myself in an Elephant's body, which caused the recent furor in your town. Quite a bother I must say."

As the Elephant spoke, I looked at its movements; delicate and dainty, quite unlike a beast used to scorching days on Savannas fending off potential lion attacks.

"How was no one able to get a photo of you?" I asked.

"Oh, that's thanks to this," the Elphant said, gesturing to the box on its head with the black wandlike instrument.

"The object is a disruptive transmitter that blocks devices from recording images of me," the Elphant said.

It moved over to a few of the boxes, waving the same wand shaped object over them periodically. It looked at me.

"And what do you do sir?"

"I am an accountant," I said.

"You don't sound very happy about that."

"Well it isn't the most glamorous job in the world," I replied.

"You should try interdimenionsal travel! You could see the sights of Cygnia 5, dive into the lava pools of E*QQQL*e*K9,* and lose yourself in the pleasure centers of Risa."

"Risa? Like the pleasure planet in the *Star Trek* series?"

"You have a fictional planet named Risa in your local literature?"

"Yes," I replied with a smile, feeling a flicker of social savvy.

The Elephant fell on the ground in a convulsive fit of laughter. It rolled around as it echoed laughs that sounded like the honking of a horn in boom after boom. I kept my distance as the massive form rolled around the floor, not once going close to any of the oblong boxes.

"I'm sorry!" the Elephant said in a choked voice. "The odds of that are so statistically improbable it made me giddy with laughter."

I sat on the ground near the Elephant. My heart was racing. In front of me, the talking Elephant that knew everything about astrophysics and pleasure planets slowly regained its composure.

"Where I'm from, there is nothing funnier than statistical improbability," the animal said.

"I see."

"I thank you for that. I was quite annoyed with this wrong body mess up, and I wasn't looking forward to vaporizing you either."

I stood up in a stance of both fear and anger.

"What do you mean! Vaporize me?"

"Well I'm giving you priveleged information. Humans won't actually be able to deal with interdimensional travel for some time, and the universal rules mandate that all such travel must be done anonymously. Should someone find out I'm from another dimension, or discover my travel array, either I or a representative from the company will vaporize them to preserve universal integrity."

I looked around, frightened.

"Don't worry, that joke alone was enough preserve your essence, and there is no way for the company to monitor me between dimensions."

"Doesn't that bother you? The idea you'd have to kill someone who accidentally found out about you?"

The Elephant sat up into a sitting position, crossed its lower legs and motioned with a massive foreleg for me to do the same. I sat back down, my heart still beating fast in my chest. There was no idea in my mind how the Elephant would have vaporized me, and I didn't want to find out either.

"Where we are from, we understand that one's essence is continuous. I wouldn't be harming the real you, just the shell you are in."

"Shell?"

"Shell, body, whatever you call it. In my hometown we change bodies all the time. Although if I vaporized you, you'd be in cosmic limbo for however long it took for humans to figure out essence transplants, so I can see how that could be somewhat inconvenient."

My head spun with the data. I tried visualizing these far off places, and what a "essence transplant" machine would even look like.

"So I won't *kill* you as you say," the Elephant said. "In fact, feel free to ask me a few questions. I'm getting ready to leave anyway."

"Why did you come here?" I asked.

"A friend recommended the place," the Elphant said with another chuckle. "That friend said you guys had some infectious music called Ragga or Reggae and that I absolutely MUST experience it."

My eyes grew wide. "Are you serious?"

"Isn't this the land of reggae? I actually prefer dancehall music myself. My friend brought some back to my dimension and it was a riveting listen. I love when you guys play that fog horn sound when you are mixing your tracks."

The Elephant stood on its legs raised one foreleg in the air and shouted: "BAP! BAP! BAP!"

The words were like thunder in my ears, but I couldn't stop laughing. Just like the animal before I rolled in convulsions of laughter. When I sat back in my former position, I saw the animal seated the same way as before.

"So you've listened to Jamaican music," I said

"Oh yes, in fact this isn't my first trip, which is why I'm so annoyed. I made sure to come on a Tuesday evening, had a room ready at a nearby hostel and I was all set to go to Weddy Wednesdays and all the street dances. But of course as an Elephant this is impossible. In fact the body I'd chosen was supposed to sort of look like you."

We sat in silence for some time, the low hum of the boxes around us creating a pulsing, harmonic rhythm.

"What do you love about the culture?" I asked.

"Oh the release of course. All that noise and dancing, drinking red rum, and dancing all night. Where I'm from we don't procreate the same way you see, so it's good that I get to let loose once in a while."

"You mean sexually?"

"Yes!" the Elephant replied with another laugh. "I travel with what you'd call a 'creation device'. I generate a lot of what you humans call money and have a grand time."

"Oh?"

"Yes, it didn't take me very long to understand that spending ridiculous amounts of money on the female species allows me to often engage in entering their pleasure centers."

Another rolling wave of laughter held me in a tight grip.

"So on this trip I was booked to take some dance classes, meet some new girls and enter their pleasure centers, smoke some weed and then go back home."

The Elephant sighed again. "I am quite annoyed."

"So why can't you get another body and come back?"

The Elephant leaned to one side, resting it's jaw and tusk on the ground.

"Time my boy, time. Interdimensional travel is expensive and time consuming. When I go back I'll have to explain what happened, get some of my investment back and book another slot, which might take several years."

"Years?"

"Well years in your time. I don't see time the way you do, but regardless, it is still inconvenient."

The animal gracefully eased itself up and stood on two legs again.

"Well I have to get going," it said to me.

The animal crooked it's head upwards and to the left as if thinking about something, then said in a perfect Jamaican accent, "*Bless up*."

I stood there in a wave of shock and confusion.

"I understand if this can significantly affect how you view your life from this point on. Would you like me to vaporize you if you can't handle it?"

"Of course not!" I retorted.

"Ah very nice," the Elephant said with a chuckle. "What I'll do is, when I get my slot back, I'll look you up."

"Do you know where I live?" I asked.

"You humans and your simple information," the animal replied.

It waved the wand that had been in its trunk this entire time over a few more boxes. The boxes made the same rhythmic humming noises, but slightly faster.

"Okay the frequency that will take me back to where I am is amplifying, so you'll need to leave. The trip destroys whatever body I'm in, so technically if you were to follow me you'd lose your present body."

"Could I follow you?" I asked.

"Absolutely not," the Elephant replied. "First of all you'd be an illegal alien. Secondly, we'd have nowhere to house you and I don't think you'd find the creatures on my planet in the least aesthetically pleasing. Then there's the whole problem of having three sex organs."

"Three?"

"Maybe the next time we speak, we'll get into that, but for now, cheers. Just walk the way you came and it is important that you don't look back. After you pass the last black box, you'll be allright."

In this moment I caught the Elephant's eye, which was diameter of a small drum. It nodded at me and I nodded back, turned and started walking forward. The humming noise increased around me with each step I took, and I felt the fear again. Why couldn't I look back? I didn't want to know. I was about twenty boxes closer to the original one I had passed and the humming noise filled the area around me, beautiful and hypnotic. When I passed the last box, the noise suddenly stopped and for a split second, I wasn't sure, but I swore I heard the Elephant singing an old Bob Marley song. Silence fell around me and I closed my eyes for a few moments. When I looked around the darkness was gone. Sunlight shone clearly through the high windows of the National Arena spreading across its vast breadth, showing no signs of either the array, or the Elephant. I sat where I was for a few minutes, processing the information I'd just learned. My watch read three-thirty. I groaned, thinking of the caterpillar of traffic already on the road, waiting for me. I walked outside the arena, back into the bright light of day, and went home.

Pews of the Night

It is another night where we kneel at pews in the belly of the city; accepting offerings of sake dropped on eagerly sucking tongues as we wish to rise unscathed from the ashes of sin in the morning. I leave the opulent hotel and go up the macadamized road with my friend Mark who is visiting me in Japan. I do not call Tokyo home but know it well, having lived in nearby Chiba for the last three years. We walk amidst the glow of incandescent lights, some hanging from wires above us, some glaring with contempt from the ubiquitous windows of convenience stores packed with questionable bento. It is a Friday night like any other, where we will become lost in the stream of memories and fragmented images that make up the stitched composite of a weekend life; seeing faces red with the tint of inebriety, men and women dancing around each other in vodka-soaked double-entendres, and the idle few, the modern *Ronins* with no sword or master, slave to the call of the night.

Our conversation is an important one. I am extolling the virtues of my favourite drink, Suntory Strong. I stand in the best forum for its espousal, a convenience store, one of tens of thousands that dot street corners and insatiable night owls.

"You are always drinking this, why?" he says to me.

I pull a long, heavy can from one of the fridges in the rear of the store, I like its weight in my hand, the quantity of its liquid contents signaling a pleasurably, ambivalent portent.

"It isn't like beer," I say. "There isn't all that mess of suds in your belly, making you all puffy and what not. It goes down smooth and easy, and it's 8.5 percent alcohol, so with just a handful of these, you are set for the night."

Processing my words, I see him calculating the night in his eyes; the entry fees for clubs and the growing tally for light beers and poorly mixed drinks. I see the reflections in his irises of the women we'd meet and hear the playback of our future dialogue; the chorus of questions about names and birthplaces, statements about cute dresses, compliments about stiletto shoes and soft purses, the touch of delicate fingers against our respective forearms, and the possible return home with a complete stranger.

"All right then, Suntory it is," he says.

We pay for the drinks and head back into the night. It is a night that I like, clean and sharp, like the undulating edges of the skyline, aplomb in its visual staccato. It is a fall night, and I relish the pleasant cool, tingling my skin with each step. The name of the club we go to isn't important, nor are its occupants. All I remember are the stark lights scarring my retinas in quick bursts, a handsome bartender giving me a free drink, and a girl whispering something to me before kissing me on the cheek only to return to a table with her boyfriend. My friend is a blur in this recollection as well, as I see him smiling and chatting with girls of indiscriminate appearance and talking to me about topics that change every forty seconds as we drink away the illusion that we are not boring people. Then we leave the club, our gaits hampered by the sake, vodka and rum, and make the long walk back to train station. First, we stop somewhere, anywhere, a McDonald's, a falafel house, a ramen shop, and eat to slowly adjust our discordant equilibrium back to acceptable levels. When we exit, we are whole again, ready for the day and the night, with its repeated routine of sexual trial and error. We go into the train now, greeted by the sallow lights and other bipedal remnants of the night like us. There are many people aboard, and for a moment we observe a moment of silence. We are either tired or have nothing to say, lost in a gap of time in the same way the train blasts through a black pocket of tunnel with no lights. The unsuccessful night usually leads to us having wandering eyes at this time, because there might be a girl on the train who is friendly and untainted by the sleaze of the night before, ready to dive into the arms of either one of us, despite the liquor on our breath. My friend taps me on the shoulder, and gestures to a man near us.

"Yo, that guy, does he know that girl?"

A young attractive woman in a black skirt is standing two feet way from me, flanked by a man in a sharp suit holding a briefcase. The man is leaning into her with his chest and neck slightly arched forward, out of rhythm with how everyone else is standing. The woman does not seem bothered by the man's proximity.

"I don't know, they are standing a bit close, so probably they know each other," I muse.

But then, I see the stirrings of discomfort rise in the woman's face; a visible tension in her eyes from a slight squint accompanied by a crunching of her shoulders that emphasizes her need to be like stone, unbothered by human things, an object to be observed and not touched. She moves slightly to the left, but the man matches her rhythm, even as the train groans and sways with the stress of taking a rapid corner. They do this somber dance for a minute or so; the man pressed against her left side, the woman halfway between movement and complete immobility. Then the train comes to a stop, and the woman exits quickly, leaving the man standing where he was.

My friend immediately begins to laugh. Pressing in an obvious outline in the man's right pant leg, is the visible swell of his erect penis. It points downward and to the left, resembling a clock face with the short arm displaying a time of four o'clock. We stand there, towering expatriate paragons, and laugh at him mercilessly. The man makes no effort to hide his erection, but instead stands there for a moment, calmly holding his suitcase, and takes a brief step out onto the train tracks. He looks to the left and right casually, returning to his position before the doors close.

"Guess he's trying to find another one!" my friend says with another hooting laugh.

I am sure he hears this, but he ignores us, his face serious and lacking. As the train moves on again, I imagine this man prowling the cars at night, standing behind the right kind of woman, getting close, just close enough to turn into the Yoji man, Mr. four o'clock, trying to impossibly push his pecker through a world of fabric into confines of anonymous women. He is out there amidst the dark streets and its even darker underbelly, known only by those who have seen him in person, or the stippled representation lurking in an officer's box. We laugh at Mr. four o'clock and his delicate perversion. We laugh at the way he feigned a projected familiarity with the young woman, how one would remarkably not know that burning beneath the stoic veneer of a tired face, was a burning, pulsing thing in his pants. This more than anything, is our memory of the night, most of which was already lost in the depths of several drinks and the usual menagerie of glassy-eyed women. Women looking for a man good at what the Yoji man does, by feigning the right kind of interest, painting a lie for the world to see and ultimately accept.

TODAY

Shibuya streets scream in a warbled gasp as we announce our presence. Touts and idlers ignore us like stains on the sidewalk, because we are part of this world, affixed to things like tattered posters and the idea that tomorrow will be the same as it was yesterday. We have however, attracted the attention of another type of night watcher, those driven out into the shadow like roaches when the light switch clicks, roaches with heels and purpose. The first prostitute, leathery and aged with use, grabs my arm. I wince at her touch, feeling not a palm on my skin but living sandpaper, a hand made for sculpting or building houses, not offering services for two thousand yen in the dark of night.

"Do you want massage?" she asks.

"No thanks," I say.

"Only two thousand yen. Come now, we go to second floor."

She points a scary finger upward to building so dirty and of ill repute it would make shadows afraid of the dark.

"Seriously I'm good," I reply.

Beside me, the same thing is happening to Mark. My attaché is a leathery, aged thing, but her counterpart is young with a cherubic face and intelligent eyes. She is out of place here, with her innocent good looks, fit more for a soap commercial than the occupation of lady of the night. Soon, we are able to release ourselves from the clutches of their aggressive advances, and continue into the night.

THREE HOURS EARLIER

I sit in a pasta shop somewhere in Shibuya, chatting to a dancer that resembles a perfect ten model. I am assaulted by powerful brown eyes and body of golden skin bundled in a top that fights to hold her generous bosom in, her legs barely guarded by a skirt far too short to hide her thighs. The name of this exquisite creature is Jeri, and her mission in town is to dance in a show somewhere in Roppongi. Despite the large visual catalogue I have of women I've met, I concur with a nod from my friend and his lascivious gaze that she is one of the hottest women I've met since I've been to Tokyo. Like the constant bedlam and glowing buildings around us, she is a stark thing of unusual interest, forged from something inhuman, born fully whole.

"I'm from L.A, but the scene is really good here. I might come back," she says.

I take another meandering look at her, wearing an innocent straw hat and that traffic-stopping skirt, the unblemished, hypnotic skin.

"I did this show," she says. "With a Japanese group called the PEOPLE EATERS."

"Sounds bizarre," I say with a laugh.

Jeri, Mark and I chat about traveling and our adventures for a few minutes. Mark regales her with tales of his many incredible outings in New York, in particular a few poignant incidents with coke-fueled supermodels attempting to pull him into public bathrooms. I take a lighter route, chatting about a story where I got stuck in an Airport on the way to France and met an ultra famous writer, the name of whom I cannot remember. She laughs with the affected tone of one who is constantly hearing vivid stories from a sea of faceless men like us.

"What are you guys doing tonight?" she asks.

"Maybe Roppongi or here in Shibuya," Mark replies.

She giggles at the mention of Roppongi.

"I'm performing tonight at this place called The Gallery in Roppongi," she says. "You guys should check it out."

Jeri, it turns out is a professional Go-Go dancer. To me this would explain her exquisitely toned body, but the title has confused Mark, who needs to clarify what exactly a Go-Go dancer is. I must admit, I did not know the difference either, and was curious to find out.

"Is Go-Go dancing stripping?" he asks in a genuine voice.

"No, its not," she says, with a little bit less of the wind in her sails.

I beam my best smile at her, the one I reserve for the end of the night when I have nothing else, save a smile and the potential that the girl across from me may respond to it, because I have run out of words. Slapping Mark on the back, I chide him.

"Come on man! Not every woman who dances on an elevated platform is a stripper," I say with a chuckle.

Jeri laughs, loud like clear bells. We exchange numbers and she stands up, off to her next destination. I am surprised at how petite she is, and desire to see her in action, laced with glitter and strobe lights. She exits into the Tokyo melee outside, vanishing.

"Wow, what are the odds of meeting a girl like her randomly like that?" I say.

"I guess that's Tokyo for you," Mark replies with a laugh.

He had seen her previously loitering in front of a man's stall, idly considering his wares for purchase. The merchant was a complete shadow of a human being, bereft of both color in his face and clothes, with skin so loose it looked like he took it off at night. I suggested he say hello to this woman, and her positive response led us to the nearby café. After last night and today, Mark is a different man. His Tokyo is not supposed to be this. His was a trip designed for an elderly couple traveling on the last fumes of their youthful expectations. Itineraries like his involved slow passage through sleepy temples, semi-famous sushi restaurants and visual romps at sites like the Tokyo Tower. He did not know about the Shibuya arena and it's endless concert with thousands of fans. He did not predict that buzz your brain feels when you are thrust into a hive mind; a dot on a living work of pointillism, where infinity is in front of you at all times. That vista of troops of people wading about in a sea of bodies, so many lives in front of you all at once. This is not a life in the woods, where a man with a hairy chest forages for food, followed by a gang of scruffy children in his wake. We forage through concrete streets and dark bars with nothing behind us save the delicious past we create. I am a child of this world, a slave to its lights and drama, but he is adamant that we take some part in his itinerary and I nod in agreement, strolling back into the clamor to assist in finding a revolving sushi restaurant somewhere in the vicinity.

A friendly African tout gives him directions and we trot through streets exploding with light until we arrive at our destination. It isn't large or small, but somewhat cramped and nigh full to capacity. Mark let's out an uncharacteristic squeal of excitement.

"This is it! Tokyo!" he says with gusto.

As we enter, a wrinkled Japanese man in a pristinely white outfit wearing a chef's hat points to a sign at the reception area written in English which reads: *You must eat at least seven dishes.* Each dish had one roll of sushi, made in real time and put onto an endlessly revolving conveyer belt that a customer picks up and eats at their leisure.

"That's cool with me," I say.

We are ushered to a few seats around the back, near a small aquarium with fish that appear to be completely lifeless. I do not have time to determine whether they are real or not, because I recognize someone there. He possesses that famous look, an actor perhaps. I turn on the charm and ask him if he is a 'professional actor'. He smiles with perfect movie star teeth and says he is.

"I love your work," I say, forgetting his name.

Though I do not patronize these types of establishments often, the sushi here is excellent. We serve our bodies well with eight and nine plates respectively. Beside me, a few feet away, The Actor is sitting with an extremely attractive woman. They seem relaxed, and I fantasize about their conversation. Did he meet her on the way here? Was it the type of spontaneous trip that a Hollywood millionaire could make on a whim? Or were they just friends? She could teach English here in Tokyo and they could have known each other since high school, or she could be his newest femme fatale, another notch on a belt with little space for new victories. Alas, I would never know. We say goodbye to the restaurant and it's lovely décor and I look back for a second, trying to determine if the fish in the tank were real. Mark says they were and I am inclined to agree and almost go back to see if he or I was right, but our steps have already taken us far from the restaurant and Shibuya and her wiles have already begun to distract me.

I suggest going to this bar called Gas Panic, a surefire den of decadence and cheap alcohol guaranteed to generate some kind of interesting story. My last encounter of note there was with a surly English teacher from Australia who consistently referred to Japanese people as 'Japs' and loathed whatever life he was living here in the East. Naturally, I was baffled by his attitude, but not completely shocked. There were many people living in Tokyo that were not Japanese who seemed to absolutely hate it, but were stuck to her bosom unable to remove their lips from her generously providing teat.

I explain to my friend that I am a night owl, and I feed on its energy. For him, he says that because he has no command of the language he did not even consider the possibility of an encounter with a woman while here for a few days. Ancient sites, delicious food and funky terrain were his top priority. Laughter escapes me like caged wolf.

"You'd be surprised at what can happen even without command of the language," I say to him. "One does not need fluency to have fun."

We step into the bloody red-lit murk of Gas Panic and I see his body language change. Bodies move in thick unison to pounding music. With each flash of the club's light a new cute face emerges from the moving mass. Fascinated, Mark stares at a set of women with processed hair, done in the style of Afros. They dance expertly to the music in perfect rhythm.

"They dance like black people!" Mark exclaims.

I laugh, noting how bizarre it must seem to him. This for me is nothing new, having witnessed such things dozens of times while living in Japan including *Ganguro,* girls with tans so fake and heavy it weighs on the eyes, their makeup and hair something straight out of an LSD trip. But it must be shocking for him, his first glimpse into the multicultural underbelly of a culture represented in the media by spotty stories about panty dispensers and creepy game shows. Now this image has been shattered, and Mark busies himself throwing back beers and chatting to cute girls in the herd of people thrashing about to pulsing electronic music. I have not committed fully to the night yet and sip on a light drink, seeing previous versions of myself in Mark's growing, ecstatic mania. I see where it is going.

TEN MINUTES LATER

He kneels in the bathroom, hurling up a mish mash of beer and sushi in a violent stream. I can tell he is not quite inebriated, but a victim of excess liquid in his stomach. This has also happened to me before. I believe it is the rapid, unbalanced ratio of beer to food that causes the stomach to protest angrily in these instants. On several occasions I have thrown up after drinking a beer too quickly, noting to myself afterwards that I am essentially drinking a quarter liter of bubbly foam that humans have no practical use for in their stomachs. Mark gets up with a sprightly step and washes his face. The bathroom is tiny and covered explosively in stickers, paraphernalia and stains of mysterious origin. After wiping his face with a paper towel, Mark reverts to his previous energy level.

"Definitely had too much liquid," he says to me.

"It's fine," I say, pointing at the toilet to our right. "We all get there at some point, kneeling in front of the pews of the night."

"Pews of the night! You are hilarious," Mark replies.

"Let me teach you a little Japan trick," I say.

We exit the bar and go to a convenience store. I squint in its bright light; momentarily distracted by a pair of young men both dressed immaculately like Elvis Presley. I take a brown bottle from one of the shelves and hand it to Mark.

"What's this?" he asks.

"It's called *Ukon,*" I reply. "It brings you back from the depths of any amount of alcohol you've had to drink."

"I'm not drunk though," Mark says.

"Even better, drink this and you won't even *get* drunk," I say with the assertion of a man who has tested this empirically.

He murmurs in agreement and I also buy a bottle, relishing the supercharge I know it will give me for the night ahead. Tokyo does not disappoint us as we exit the convenience store. We float across a live runway of well-dressed women and fashionable men. It is a sensual overload of the best kind; spontaneously interrupted by our high fives and screams to the night sky. We decide to take things to Roppongi and go to the train station. The song of a digital Japanese voice sings as we enter its cool innards. Two girls nearby are talking about my shoes while pointing in my direction.

"Big eh?" I say to them in Japanese.

One of them giggles, but does not look at me and resumes whatever conversation they were having. The ride comes to an end and we exit the terminal. The train does not have the opportunity to leave before a face I have seen before immediately enamors me. She is tall and lithe, with shoulder length hair. Though she wears a simple top and fitted jeans, she is a vision. Her name is Miki, whom I'd met sometime before, in the faded dregs of an event just before the sun decided to show its face. She greets me with a squeal of excitement. Her long, gorgeous arms wrap around me for a moment, and I savor the touch. Wherever she was going is now irrelevant apparently, as she leaves the platform with us.

We stroll into a club nearby. In minutes we have our own little corner at the top bar. Drinks come hard and fast, our glasses clink and I do cheers with strangers. Miki samba dances to a Justin Timberlake song with a man half her size. Time passes and the music is good, Mark is back to full form, restored and at the ready, with his third drink in hand. I suggest that Miki come with us to the next spot, but she declines with a smile and a kiss to my cheek. She is going surfing in the morning and can't be out too late. I fail to hide my disappointment and bid her adieu, watching her leave like a gazelle moving across a dark savanna. Mark catches the eye of an old, grizzled Japanese woman bursting with feral energy. She has already left three men breathless and fatigued from dancing, and seeks her fourth victim. I ask Mark if he'd be willing to truly have a wild Tokyo story and he laughs.

"One more drink, and that'd probably be it," he replies.

"Well I'm glad you didn't have that drink!" I exclaim.

This moment consumes us and we erupt into pleasant laughter. Now we are back on the street, near a McDonald's. I cannot find a place called The Gallery on my phone, nor do any of the touts seem to know where it is, though I do not believe them. An image of Jeri briefly comes to mind, the beautiful skin and gorgeous teeth. A man with incredible energy introduces himself as Joe and spins a fabulous tale of a nearby strip club with unlimited girls and drinks for one price. Idly, we entertain his claim and enter a dingy club with a gaggle of older women in tired lingerie with zero clientele. Now we are back on the street, near a McDonald's. Mark touches me.

"Do you see that?" Mark says.

I glance up and see two girls about twenty feet away looking back at us. I realize they had been following us for a few minutes, but at a distance.

"Should we talk to them? " I say.

"You better take one for the team because I'm not," Mark says.

I saw his dilemma. Of the two girls one was far more portly with a somber, distracted expression on her face. Still, this was Tokyo. I waved for them to come over and they did so, coasting on a sea of laughs and giggles. They wore matching black and white outfits and wore gray backpacks. This, naturally, was odd. The bigger one started asking us a range of questions.

"You guys kept looking back at us, so we were wondering what was going on," I say to the larger one.

"I'm sorry, my sister here was interested in you, but she doesn't speak English," she replies.

"Oh?" I reply. "What language does she speak?"

"Greek," The girl says.

"Do you need Windex?" Mark asks immediately.

The girl gives him a strange look.

"I'm joking, I'm joking. I know that statement was mad ignorant," Mark says with a laugh.

I laugh along with him, not knowing it would be a week before I realized he was referring to the pop-culture phenomenon that previously was *My Big Fat Greek Wedding*. The girl introduces herself as Athena and her sister as Mina. Though Mina apparently spoke no English, it improved by leaps about bounds within minutes of meeting us. Three tall, bedraggled drag queens stormed past, glancing at us with fiery eyes. The sisters ask us If we want to hang out. I say okay and we walk towards a bar I've been to before. A hush falls over us as we walk in silence, the Greek sisters and their strange new companions. Within seconds of entering the establishment, a man skips and hops over to us and asks us what we are drinking. The girls quietly move to a corner of the room, backpacks still on.

"One minute," I say to the server, turning to Mark.

"Dude, you think these girls are hustling us?" I ask.

He shrugs his shoulders.

"Maybe dude. Their accent changes, the weird backpacks, the Greek names and everything feel wrong. Let's bounce."

We exit the bar and the girls do not move as we do so, barely visible in the darkness of the corner they still sit in, unmoving and silent. Our hotel is a few blocks away, up a sharp slope flanked by apartment buildings. We decide to call it a night, standing by a stoplight with an unusually flaming red light. A small pair of hands grab my arm and I turn to see the prostitute from before. This time, it was the attractive one. Sandpaper hands was doing her best to regale Mark with the promise of her abilities through crinkled lips.

"I'm sorry, we go back to the hotel now," Mark said.

The light changed to green and we crossed, hearing a voice behind us scream: "I come to hotel with you!"

We laugh and turn the corner, but then my phone buzzes. It is a text from Jeri.

You still coming? The place is on 6-Chome beside a coffee shop named Rita's. Hope to see you! I go on in a few minutes XXX

FIVE MINUTES LATER

Jeri stands on a platform adorned in nothing but gold and string, her body dripping with glitter. The backdrop for her performance, where she and two other girls dance is a massive projector with vibrating lines pulsing in an array of colors. Seeing her before in the pasta shop was a twist of fate, a reminder that in a harsh world there are beautiful things. Now she was truly a dream, her curves and motions a kick to the senses, brighter than all the lights behind her. The audience shares my sentiments, awestruck with each move of her body, the flawless execution a marvel as her high heels and hair flail about like confetti.

She meets us after the show and we have drinks at the bar. I marvel at her drinking prowess, downing shot after shot. The glitter still on her face and arms causes her to sparkle like a diamond. Jeri has a friend, another exotic lookalike that forces me to accept that it isn't all a dream, that this must be real, this adventure with Mark and I. Our energies mingle positively and we decide to take the night elsewhere. We stroll four strong up the Roppongi main street. Alcohol protects us in an invisible carapace; the world is ours. We are invulnerable to all outcomes and completely fearless. Mark reminds me we have ample liquor in our hotel room, which is a vast behemoth of marble, with multiple bedrooms. I communicate this verbatim to Jeri, who squeezes my hand in agreement. Mark is in good form; Jeri's friend bursts out frequently in laughter, tickled by whatever he is whispering in her ears. We are back at the stoplight, where the prostitute grabbed my arm sometime before. A noise alerts us. About ten feet away, by a wall a man kneels, heaving up his entire life in a growing puddle of milky vomit.

"Gross," says the girl with Mark, hugging him.

We all look at him for a few seconds before turning back to the light. Then, Mark looks at me and we both erupt into laughter, sending our voices far above us, dashing through skyscrapers and bouncing of windowpanes. The laughter is infectious and even the ladies laugh with us as we cross the street, into the shadow of an overpass. I laugh so hard I cannot breathe and Mark has tears in his eyes. We struggle to compose ourselves as the women look at us with a bemused gaze. Soon oxygen returns to my lungs and my stomach is no longer cramped with its convulsive effort. I loop Jeri's hand back into the crook of my arm, and Mark does the same with her friend. Jeri pinches me, smiling at me with those exquisite teeth, asking me what the joke is as we walk away, the man far behind us now, still kneeling by the wall.

Misses Cats

I wish I could have seen John Lennon in concert; watching screaming crowds of girls and guys with bowl haircuts and men in business suits rush to the stadium from work to catch the Beatles in Japan for the first time. I could imagine myself, young and thin in a white t-shirt with a peace sign on it, screaming so loudly I couldn't speak for a week afterward. I wish for things sometimes in the quiet moments, when I stare at nothing and my eyes are open, but all I see are my thoughts. I am Thirty-five years old.

I live in Hamamatsu, a small city in Shizuoka, and it is a cold and rainy day. All around the city, glittering drops fall like dots of mercury to the Earth. My hair, black and short, is a little wet. I'm riding my bike slowly somewhere near my house. I see a blur flash past. In front of me, rapidly moving forward on a bike is a person of African descent. I watch him disappear down the road, pumping his pedals in fast even strokes. I smile to myself, and think of a time when the entire town would have paused if they saw him. Cars would stop and people would follow the young man to his house. They would probably want to touch his skin, feel his hair and pepper him with questions. But not now.

I breathe slowly as I approach my destination. In front of me is a local shop. I come here sometimes to buy food. An older woman in town told me about the old markets, with squat broad-chested women selling their wares in high pitched voices, and her as a little girl running through the stalls, grabbing fat fruits and vegetables to put in her mother's basket.

"My hair was long then," she said. "It was down to my back, and everywhere I went the older women would touch it, chanting sweet compliments."

I tried to imagine her at the time, small and fearless, with sharp eyes and a tiny nose, running through a sea of towering legs. Now supermarkets are massive warehouses bathed in white light, with temperature controlled climates. When the doors swish open a voice from nowhere tells you 'good day, happy shopping!' and attendants move so quickly you rarely get to look in their eyes. I don't hear the tinkling of bicycle bells and the slap of slippers on the ground. Maybe that's what the old lady used to hear.

Behind the supermarket is an aqueduct, and beside that, a parking lot. I happened to ride through the lot one day on my way to the supermarket, when I saw them: a group of little rogues, bundles of gray and black hair, green eyes and sharp teeth. They were smaller then, a stray set of little cats used to a life outside. They looked at me with no expression when I first saw them. I was in their territory, their world. I stopped my bike that day, feeling my knees creak as my feet touched the earth, and I smiled. In a pouch beside me, I had the last bits of a sandwich I ate for lunch.

"Chuda," I said. "Come and eat, Chuda."

I stooped over slightly, watching the cats watch me. They were used to a harsh world of fighting, loud noises and cold places, they had no trust in their hearts. One cat, which I named Masao, bore the marks of that life. A vertical scar ran over his left eye, and between the soft hairs on his body, you could see the crisscross patterns of old wounds from dozens of fights. Still, Masao looked calm and collected, regal as cats always do. Chuda never came to me that day, Masao did. He reared up on all fours, stretching and yawning. Then he paced around a few times, turning his back to me and fluffing his fur. He approached fearlessly and stopped a few feet from my outstretched hand. I tossed the sandwich on the parking lot and he pounced on it, ravenously tearing at small pits of pork and bread. Masao ate everything, hissing viciously at the other cats that dared to take an interest in his dining. Every cat had the name of someone I knew. Masao was the name of the first man I ever loved.

Nineteen years ago, I was a rebel. I called myself a product of post-westernized Japan, after the new waves of fashion and music had long swept up on its shores. I lived in Tokyo then, and at sixteen I was brutally outgoing, argumentative and sexually curious. I had no patience for the ways of my world. I read about America from magazines I smuggled home from a small shop near an Army base. I loved the Smashing Pumpkins and started learning English from Archie comics. In high school I was a terror for the teachers, who thought I was irredeemable. I paid no attention in class, flirted with the boys and was constantly berated by the principal.

"A woman must know her place!" he barked at me once.

I was even slapped in the face when I called a teacher an idiot. I smile as I remember this person; my opinion still hasn't changed. When my father got word of what had happened, he had shouted at me until the *tatami* mats in our house trembled. In the 50's, he said, such disobedience would probably result in terrible circumstances. "Fuck the 50's, "I told him, and went to my room.

My job then was a part-time assistant at an old record store in Akihabara. There I could lose myself for a few hours a day in a closed-eye escape; walking through the meadows of my mind under a pair of Sony headphones. My English was horrible, but most of the time, I figured out what the songs were trying to say. Many nights I sat with Mr. Hirada the owner, discussing the finer points of American and Japanese culture. He would tell me dirty jokes and pinch me on my buttocks when I messed up an order. He said he loved blonde women and secretly wished to see blonde pubic hair. His car was Japanese but he wanted a Mustang. He even said he met one of the Beatles at the big fish market in Tsukiji, which I found hard to believe. Sometimes he would give me free records, or send me home with a bottle of Sake and make me promise to bring it back the next day unopened. He was strange but I could relax around him. In the record store, the world outside wasn't screaming at me, I was simply me. Mr. Hirada's daughter Miko worked in the store from time to time. She was mostly quiet and blank, spending most of her time studying at the counter.

"She wants to go to Harvard," Mr. Hirada said proudly.

Business most days was slow and the shop could get quite boring. I would read trashy novels that made me blush and chew on snacks while I memorized album lyrics. It would be almost twenty years before I realized how badly I was saying the words to the songs I sang in my Japanese accent. On one of these days, when the store was almost empty and Mr. Hirada was out picking up a delivery, I met Masao. He came in larger than life, standing well over six feet tall with a face I never forgot. Beside him, was an attractive young woman dressed in very stylish clothing. Without even knowing who she was, in seconds I was intensely jealous of her.

"Got any of the Beatles?" he had asked.

"I think so," I replied.

As I walked through the aisles of the store, I snuck peeks at him between the sliced lenses of album covers on the shelves. The girl seemed bored and uninterested in music, but Masao was fascinated. He asked me what seemed like a thousand questions and a few times, he stood close enough for me to smell him. The scent reminded me of an enclave of calm trees by a lakeside. I felt my anger at his girlfriend turn into a desire, a desire to learn more about him. I found the album and they left. He was only in the store for a few moments, but my entire world was invaded by his presence. The twitches of his eyebrows and the slightest hint of a smile curling on his lips rung in my heart like a thousand bells. A week later, I saw him again, this time he was alone.

He wanted another album, this time from Eikichi Yazawa. As I walked to an aisle with a mixture of Japanese and American rock, I saw him twirling a lock of his hair with his right hand. I would learn eventually this meant he was nervous.

"Do you mind if I ask you what your name is?" he asked.

I laughed.

"No I don't mind. My name is Haruna," I replied.

"You think Eikichi's cool?"

"I can't give my opinion unless I know your name," I replied.

"Oh, I'm sorry! My name is Masao," he said.

"Okay Masao, I think Eikichi's pretty cool. Sexy too," I said.

He chuckled and muttered under his breath about women and rock stars.

"Where's your girlfriend?" I asked him, my heart fluttering slightly.

"From the last time? Oh, that was Ayako. She was just a friend," he replied flatly.

On our first date we had ice cream at a shop near where I lived. That day he wore green slippers and a black t-shirt that read 'REVOLUTION!' in bold red letters. We ate vanilla ice cream until we were sick, and I laughed until the summer evening turned into a black night. Masao was from a wealthy family that worked with car companies to develop assembly line robots and machines. He was well traveled and spoke very good English, though I couldn't understand much of what he said whenever he chose to speak it. He said he 'dug my vibe', making me laugh. I didn't know what it meant, but it sounded cute. I fell for him instantly, and I found my usual teenage anger shifting into a wild, new, something else. I spoke to him about my emotionally distant parents, and my hidden love for small animals. We went to a lot of zoos and parks, spending time curled up in each other's arms or under blankets, listening to the leaves flap gently around us.

The first time we made love, I cried. It was on a day his parents weren't home. After a few awkward exchanges and giggles in the kitchen, we went to his bedroom. It was overwhelmingly large, with an opulent interior décor. The black satin sheets, expensive lamps and a glimpse of the city through thin venetian blinds felt alien and exciting compared to my cramped room back home. At some point during our lovemaking I started crying. In the crescendo of my coital weeping, as fat tears fell from my eyes onto his exposed chest, I had my first orgasm.

We were only together for a few months, and I the blissful teenager, expected it to last forever. I had changed since meeting him. I had done away with my large t-shirts and ruffled pants. My long wild hair had been transformed into a cute bun and I even wore makeup, something I swore never to do. But Masao liked these things, and my love for him was crippling in its intensity. At school I had changed. I was more attentive and less disruptive. At home my parents, as robotic as they were, seemed mildly pleased with me. One day in particular my father touched me on the shoulder, pausing as if to say something, changed his mind, then walked into the kitchen. I growled under my breath, wondering how I was even born.

Then, Masao left. The reasons were not completely clear, but I heard it was his father's decision. I had met him once, briefly, and he looked at me in the way a person looks at a pebble in a shallow pool of stagnant water on the ground. Masao always told me he loved me, and that his family couldn't bully him into splitting us apart. When he left, it was a day before my birthday. I was turning seventeen and as a joke we made reservations at a restaurant with the same name. Masao didn't show up, and I sat there until the restaurant was almost empty, my only company a lukewarm decanter of tea.

The truth was different. It had nothing to do with his father. I saw him a few weeks later in Shibuya with a tall girl with dark European features and the most sensual eyes I had ever seen. I saw them from a distance, laughing at nothing. Masao, tall and resplendent in chinos and a white t-shirt seemed blissfully happy. I couldn't bear to get close, and I burned with anger. For a fleeting moment the girl caught my eye then looked away. If she told Masao I was looking at them, I never knew. He didn't turn around. I ran to the train station in a huff. That day the roaring of the train sounded like a beast from hell, cackling malevolently at my misfortune.

My devastation had no end. I destroyed my room and cut off all my hair. I had daily fights with my parents and screamed at anyone who would listen. I even lost my job at the record store, after arguing with a customer who wanted an album I had bought for Masao once that I refused to sell him. I cried everywhere; in bathrooms with my chin buried in my knees, my room as I hugged myself, and often just walking about, my face a stained mess of makeup and tears. One day, I came home and my father was sitting in the kitchen reading the newspaper. My hair was cut boyishly short and dyed deep burgundy.

"You disgrace me," he said.

That night I left the house, taking one last look at its outline on the tip of my road amidst the myriad phone wires and telephone poles. All I had was a small bag with some choice clothes and shoes with me, but in a strange way, I felt happy. That was the same night I met Chuda.

Chuda was a street hustler with an erratic demeanor. He was shorter than me with a round face, large, probing eyes and a sharp wit. He followed me for ten minutes as I walked aimlessly through Shinjuku, telling me I was beautiful and perfect and that he wanted to take care of me. Eventually I asked him one question.

"Do you know somewhere I can stay?" I asked.

"Sure," he replied.

His face looked disingenuous, and if I had been older I would have understood what the look meant, but I just wanted to run away, anywhere. That night, he took me to a small apartment somewhere near Roppongi.

"Stay here as long as you like," he said.

With that, he disappeared, leaving me in a compact room sitting on a small futon, staring at the ceiling. It would be three years before I left that place. With Chuda's help I got into a strange life, working as a hostess and sometimes as a call girl, spending time with powerful and wealthy men. My clients said I was beautiful, but I never saw it. The world felt cold and clammy, like sweaty palms on a winter's night.

In Chuda, I saw a person with two faces. At times he would morph from the sweet talking street guy to a little bundle of rage. He would get drunk and come into the apartment with a pair of girls, and scream at me to get out. Sometimes, I would wake up to see a little package on the floor by the bed: a snack or a small cake, even expensive perfume. It was obvious he had left it, but he never said anything about it. I didn't understand him but it never mattered that much, as I didn't understand myself either. Our arrangement worked. We had a relationship rooted in a mutually shared wealth of insecurity, depression and escapism. He had left home a few years before I did, the signs of the move visible in his face and eyes. He looked much older than his twenty-five years.

For a little while, I had a pet. It was a small mouse that lived somewhere behind a set of old *tatami* mats near the kitchen door. I saw it occasionally at night, popping out to rummage through our tiny garbage bin. The apartment was so small it felt like one room, and I often tried to imagine how the mouse saw things; scurrying about it had more space here than I ever would. Many nights I left food out on purpose, watching the rodent come out in the semi-darkness, gobbling it up in its little paws. Soon it came out every night in this way, and I smiled inwardly.

I woke up one night to a furious noise beside me. It was Chuda, pounding his foot on the mouse until it was a red smear. I screamed and told him to stop and he looked at me as if I was crazy.

"These things are filthy!" he said with a shout.

He left the apartment then, as I stared at the bloodstain and the creature's dismembered body, only a few feet away from where I left food for it each night.

The men I met offered me a lot of money to do sexual things, but I was too shy to volunteer, though some other girls I knew were very willing. In the bars and small restaurants I followed the men to, I wore nice black dresses, copious amounts of makeup and high heels that often made my feet bleed if I wore them too long. This is how I earned my living; my previous life like a faded picture in an old drawer. One night a client got very drunk and he told me he needed help going home. After an awkward taxi ride we came to a large apartment building in a part of Tokyo I'd never been to. We took the elevator to his residence, which was on the thirty-sixth floor. He fumbled with a strange looking electronic key and opened the door. I followed him in, trying to make out the apartment in the darkness. Within seconds I felt a blinding pain behind my neck. Later I would find that another man was in there, and he had hit me. I fell to the floor and in my semi-consciousness heard the faceless man growl with carnal pleasure. As I screamed and felt my clothes being torn off the world started to spin. I flailed at my attacker, feeling my nails dig into human flesh. The man hissed like a demon, and then I felt another sharp blow, this time to the front of my face, and all was dark.

I woke up to see the men staring at me. I had nothing on save my underwear. Horrified, I ran to the nearest room I could find, and it happened to be a bathroom. My face was a blue-black mess and my lips were swollen. My groin felt chafed and I knew what they had done to me.

"Come out, Come out," I heard the voice of my client say.

I didn't reply and stayed in the bathroom for a long time. A small window was my only view of the outside world. Thirty-six stories below, the movement of people was like seeing ants on a promenade. I thought about jumping out the window but it was impossible; it was too small. Eventually, I walked out of the bathroom with a soap dispenser. It was made of a heavy ceramic material, and felt very expensive. As the door opened, I threw it at the first person I saw. It hit his face with a dull thud, and he fell to the ground hard, not moving. My client, his large stomach like a ball, stood naked in front of me with an erection rising out of a small forest of black pubic hair between his legs. He was wielding a knife.

"Sit or I will kill you," he said.

I screamed and ran towards the door, but I felt his hand grab me. He rested the blade lightly on my arm, and I could feel how sharp it was. My legs trembled.

"Sit," he said gruffly.

I followed his instructions and walked through the apartment to a living room. It was opulent beyond belief, with exotic furniture, large paintings and some high-tech devices I didn't recognize. The man must have been extremely wealthy. He was smiling, and tapped the side of the knife against his penis.

"Touch it," he said with a low, evil laugh.

I paused and his eyes flashed with madness.

"Touch it you whore!" he said.

I heard the groans of the man on the floor behind me, and a sudden fear enveloped me. *They are going to kill me,* I thought. The pot-bellied man took a few steps forward, the blade always directly facing me. I started to cry as I held his member. His large stomach jiggled and he grunted with pleasure. Then I heard a crash. The client looked away and I pushed him forward, causing him to fall on the edge of a small table. He shrieked in pain. A voice echoed throughout the apartment. The voice was screaming my name. It was Chuda. I ran to the door in only my underwear, and hurriedly opened it. I collided with Chuda in the hallway.

"Come with me now!" he shouted.

He was with two other young men, both similar to Chuda in height and appearance, with jaded eyes and hardened faces. One of them wrapped me in his jacket, and I ran from the apartment with them, my face burning with shame. The client's voice shrieked behind us, echoing in the long, empty hallway. That is when I left Tokyo. Chuda begged me to stay and said he would sort things out, but I felt void. That day I left, Chuda watched me silently as I packed my things in a large duffle bag. He tossed a bottle of pills on the bed.

"Take those, you know, just in case," he said.

I sighed and dropped the pills in my bag. I hadn't seen a doctor, and didn't plan to.

"Where will you go?" he asked.

"I don't know," I replied.

I picked up my bag and gave him a last look before stepping out the door. He said, nothing, just staring at me with true concern in his face, until I shut the door. My nightlife had afforded me a good bit of savings, and I took all of it with me. I went to the bus station and chose a terminal at random. It happened to be going to Shizuoka. On the bus I wept, my tears partially hidden by a large pair of dark glasses that hid my facial bruises. Not many people were on the bus thankfully, and I was left to weep in peace. After a long time, we came to a small city with hills in the distance with calm, clear skies. I felt like this was the place. I stepped off the bus and entered Hamamatsu.

I'm in the parking lot again, looking at the cats. Today I don't see Masao sometimes he disappears for stretches of time. The cats lounge idly near the cars, basking in the silence of the small neighborhood. Chuda is there and a large, white and orange cat that I see occasionally. I call him Taka, after the name of my husband.

Hamamatsu is a town of factories and businesses like Yamaha and Kawaii pianos. I took at a job at another record store and found a small apartment in the city. Through some people I met, I started writing articles occasionally on American music for the local newspaper. In a few months, an editor for a local magazine contacted me, asking me if I wanted a job. I took it.

I wasn't with a man for three years after leaving Tokyo, and when I finally decided to be with someone, I wanted a gentle touch; someone kind and soft. I met Taka at a local international club, where he was very popular. He was my height, with bright eyes and a relaxed face. At first I didn't find him very attractive, but he made me feel comfortable. During the months of our courtship, I rediscovered a few things about myself sexually and emotionally. I wasn't a little girl anymore, I was a woman.

I would look at the families walk around in the parks on hot summer days, while I walked quietly by myself hidden behind a pair of dark glasses. I would sit on benches and read English classics in my free time (I had started taking classes at a local center). I also did a brief stint of surfing, which Taka loved but I didn't. I even entered a fashion competition, working feverishly with a friend to produce a few lopsided sculptures for a cultural festival. We didn't win.

We were married after two years. Taka proposed to me on the beach amongst friends. His bronzed, calm face radiated a joy that is permanently welded into my memories. Despite his small stature, he had a way of connecting people, men and women; like a living thread. After our honeymoon in Australia, we came back to town, happy to start our new lives. We argued constantly about finding a proper house. I loved my apartment, but Taka wanted children and that required a house. Many times after fierce arguments our lovemaking was so passionate the neighbours could hear us. My job at the magazine was going well, I was now the assistant editor. My English had gotten much better over the years, particularly because of the classes and my writing. One Friday night, in the fall Taka was accidentally killed by a cyclist. That was ten years ago.

That night it was as if someone put an icicle in my throat and gave me two different heads, which hurt at the same time. Everything pounded and I heard the constant, thunderous roar of my blood flowing through my heart. I was at work at the time when I got the news, and my co-workers told me I fell to the floor, screaming and clutching at things and people until I could move no more.

The accident was random. The cyclist was turning on a wet sidewalk. Taka happened to be right there, and at that moment, had dropped his wallet and bent to pick it up. The cyclist saw him and braked, but the bike slid forward, hitting Taka solidly in his neck, instantly killing him. I came home that night to my bed, and it had never felt so empty and cold. Beside my pillow were little brochures for a house we had decided on. I burned them that night.

I left my job soon after and slowly fell into despair. My body became a fragile version of what it once was. I spoke to no one, and my days felt like a record scratching in slow motion. One night I went to Nakatijima beach, outside town. I looked at the waves pounding against the tetra pods. Every year people died here, after only going out in the water for a few feet. It was chilly and I was alone. Tears streamed down my face and I started wading into the water. When it was just above my thighs, I could already feel the heavy tug of the undercurrent. The sea was black as oil and raging like an angry bull. Just a few more steps and I would disappear forever, I thought. Then I heard it: a low whine somewhere in the distance. I turned around and squinted. I heard it again, the same low whine.

About twenty feet away, I saw a small cat, walking with a few kittens beside it. As bad as I felt, I found this fascinating. The larger cat kept whining, while the little kittens idly clawed at each other. I felt something hit my leg and I stepped back in fright, thinking it was a fish. It was a dark mass bobbing in the water, a tiny bundle of clumped fur. It was a little kitten. I picked it up. Stiff and cold, it had long drowned. Its face was grim, frozen in a dead mask of pain and fright. I looked at the group of cats, getting further away in the distance and I started to wail. I sat in the water, the icy sea chilling my buttocks and soaking my pants and I held the little cat like a baby. The mother would never find it. Like Taka and so many things before me, it would be lost. I lay the cat back in the water, and watched it float up and down a few waves, finally disappearing into the black depths of the inky horizon. I got up from where I was sitting, rubbing my arms because it was so chilly, and went back home.

Until I found that parking lot by the market, I hadn't owned a cat. Maybe small creatures had become the microcosms of my life, the last bastion of my empathy. I fed these cats in torrential downpours, during searing sunny days and on cold winter nights. If I didn't see a cat, I would call its name, waiting sometimes up to an hour for it to show up. After I fed them, occasionally rubbing their heads to comfort them, I would smile, and feel happy. Then I would hop on my bike and ride home, to my apartment, the one I never left.

t.

Sleep

I don't like to sleep. Sleep they say is like being reborn, ushered into a world of light and sound, far away from the chaotic darkness of the dream world. Waking up for me is like being tossed into an endless chasm of despair. It reminds me that I am alone, walking along the large conveyor belt of life, watching it pass by. I've decided the best way to function properly, is to not sleep. If I cannot be reminded that I am re-entering a pointless existence, then I can have some semblance of normalcy. If I could just stay awake at all times, I could function wholly in the present, ever aware and watchful, like the little Buddhist statue at the foot of my bed.

I'm a model, which presumably means I'm attractive, but it's a job like any other. High on coke and pharmaceuticals, I once fell off a runway headfirst into the lap of a woman who's the CEO of large clothing company. I can't say her name, but she's well tanned and big in the fashion world. My life isn't glamorous, or is depending on how you look at it. People know me, women say hello, and I can't remember the last time I bought a drink for myself. I fell asleep in a club once, as the pulsing throb of house music made my teeth clatter. I was on a three day high of no sleep, which put me into what I call twilight. In twilight, I don't really wake up; I just sort of become hazy and re-emerge from that fuzzy space of semi-consciousness. I like it, because it doesn't remind me of the cavernous emptiness of reawakening.

At that club, I woke up with a lady beside me. She was lithe with attractive features. Her eyes were a fiery dark brown, and her skin bronzed from a life in the sun. We talked for a little while.

"What do you do?" she asked.

"I work in fashion," I replied.

"Wow, are you a model?" she said.

"Not really," I replied.

As she read between the lines her eyes gained that little

light that I'd seen dozens of times before. A drink or two later and she was saying what lots of women said:

"You are too hot for me."

"What does that mean?"

"You are too attractive for me. "

Somewhere between her next sentence and a Jay-Z song, I had left the club. I felt cold and empty. My sleeplessness had triggered and interesting side effect, a lack of appetite. Like most models I live in New York, and sometimes I lounge around the Lower East Side.

Today, I'm nibbling on a pizza crust on a corner street somewhere near First Avenue. I leave ten dollars on the table for a dollar fifty slice of pizza. I'm on day five of no sleep. The morning is cool, which is an illusion. The day will be hot and muggy and thousands will run into their air conditioned apartments and workplaces like roaches escaping bright light. Oddly, I don't sweat. I catch my reflection as I walk past an old phone booth. Little sparks of anger flash in the blackness of my mind, and just as quickly disappear. I walk for a long time. I head into a gray building somewhere in Midtown. Upstairs, I enter a small but clean studio, startlingly white.

"Hey," Ralph says.

Ralph is a photographer and Ralph is gay. Not like that matters.

"You look terrible, he says.

I nod in reply. The next four hours are a blur. A heavyset woman with a tattoo of a Care Bear on her neck applies my makeup and two people assist Ralph; both young, effeminate men. A few minutes after I arrive a chick comes in. She has high cheekbones, barely any meat on her body and striking eyes. I don't remember if I took off her shirt first.

It was in the bathroom one floor up. Her body was thin and lifeless. Sex with her was like the photo shoot; a blur of faded images and senses: cold plastic from the stall making me gasp and raising goose bumps on my arms; her tiny light blue panties hanging off the door handle; me glimpsing myself in the mirror shirtless and thin, feeling the usual spots of rage rise up to forefront of my thoughts.

"What's your name?" she asked.

I didn't answer. I was doing a line of coke off her thigh. I rose up my head.

"I'm a runway god," I said. The coke was talking, not me.

Then I laughed. I laughed until I was alone in the bathroom, and the girl and her blue panties were gone. I left the building discreetly, but everyone knew what happened. They always did. I'd get my money from the agency later.

I am awake now. The day is bright and glamorous. The clouds in the sky, puffy and white seem to be trumpeting a song with accompanying voices. Wait, those *are* trumpets. A little distance away, I see a brass band. Little kids of average looks are playing in front of a wide-open area. Union Square. I balk. Had I really walked forty blocks without realizing it? I buy a bottle of water from a street vendor and sip it.

The world is loveless, I mutter to myself.

My eyelids feel a little heavy. I walk over to a store, and stop in front of it. I look at my reflection deliberately. There I am, tall and resolute, thin and warped. The strong chin, the eyes that women say they love, I hate it all. I feel angry and depressed, alone and frightened. I also see that I'm wearing long swim trunks and a thin tee shirt: The same clothes from the photo shoot. Emotions flare throughout my body, and I am quickly awake again.

"Hey is that you?" someone says.

I turn to see a guy with broad, hairy shoulders pointing directly in front of me. I curse silently. Printed on a large banner across from us, is an image of myself and other models. It was for a campaign I had done a few months ago. In the image, I wear a light green polo shirt and dress khakis. I am smiling brightly. The smile is not real. The hairy man asks me again if it is me.

"Sometimes," I reply.

I have been functioning in this blurry way for a few months now. The lack of sleep and the faded, drug-addled walks now feel as normal as apple pie and Folgers in the morning. Somewhere near Union Square, I juggle a soccer ball with some kids while they look at me awkwardly. I don't play soccer.

I grab a cab and in minutes, I'm home. I drink coffee and call Mike. He picks up.

"Where are you?" Mike asks.

"Home," I reply.

This surprises Mike. He's been the key witness to my escalating whatever this is. I'm never home. My longest stretch has been two weeks. My apartment is frigid; I keep it that way so I don't fall asleep. I'm wearing Sponge bob pajama pants and bright yellow bunny slippers. I sip coffee.

"Are you still not sleeping?" he asks.

"Slept a little today," I reply.

"Liar! Let's grab a drink later, I've got to run," he says, his voice panting for some reason.

"Peace," I say in reply.

I look at the bunny slippers for a few minutes while I finish the coffee. I try to watch TV but it's boring. I glance at my calendar. There is a show tonight at eight. In the corner of the room, my little Buddha stares at me with closed eyes, serene and unaffected. I wish I were the Buddha.

Waking up always reminds me that I exist in a void of emptiness. I feel and smell and touch, but it just seems like stuff to pass the time while I approach my date with the Grim Reaper. I've never been into philosophy, but lately it has been tickling my mind. Has my life really been a string of bad relationships and scattered hookups?

I'm getting ready for a show I was invited to later, making sure to grab a pair of extremely snug jeans and a designer shirt. I'm prepping in the mirror, while the voice of my casting agent echoes in my mind. I can still hear his thick Jamaican accent, echoing in my mind.

"You have potential, just stay focused and it will happen," he had said.

Back then, there was nothing interesting or exotic to me about my features or the idea of a life in fashion. I was a nerdy kid with a proclivity for mood swings and trips to the local weed dealer. A part of me used to feel sorry for my agent, an ex-model who didn't get the break I did, that sub-celebrity life that's a freakish amalgam of sexual bohemia and bullheaded drive. There was a night once, a night of too much wine and weed where he made a move on me, resulting in him leaving the party with a broken nose, sprinkling the air with a stream of hot curses.

The leather of the cab's seat squawks against my buttocks as I sit down. In moments like these a mosaic of my home country pops up in front of me; the undulating streets, patches of grass in the sidewalks and the silhouette of green hills in the distance. Roads filled with scorching taxis blasting hot music and slim dark men screaming destinations to passersby in an attempt to fill their daily quota.

I tell the cabbie to take me to Soho. Skyscrapers and plush apartments flash by in lines of light and streams of bug-eyed tourists, Jewish folk walking in traditional garb, wall Street types strung out on coke and sex; and Africans selling umbrellas. I feel the pulse of this imagery shaking my body, but then I realize it's the vibration of the moving cab. Manhattan is nothing like Jamaica.

At the show, I feel great. One of the girls has coke. In a small dressing room, we talk and she suddenly breaks down and starts crying. Her boyfriend left her for a B-list actress. As she went down on me I said to her:

"That's sad."

A few walks down the runway, more steely-eyed poses and flashing lights later, the show is over. I vaguely remember talking to some press. There might have been a camera. I don't have memories lately, just fragments of broken images and sensations. The coke is fading by now, but I am still smiling a little. The event has good energy. It is sponsored by a large cosmetics company with a French name I cannot pronounce. One of the higher ups hands me an armband that gives me V.I.P access to the after party. Then, I see her.

She is strikingly beautiful, with long hair that looks hand-polished, and a face of beauty from another world. Tall and copper-skinned from her Asian heritage, she lights the room up and wows her audience with well-practiced, delicate strides. Her dress swishes to reveal her ample legs, while camera lights *pop pop pop* and the occasional voice calls to her. There she is kissing Ralph on the cheek. There she floats in a cascade of perfect laughter and teeth with some of the higher ups and VIPs. She smiles that heartbreaking smile. I almost melt. She comes near to me, arms clasped in the hairy crook of a short stocky man. He is her new boyfriend. He certainly isn't as good looking as I am, but in this world that sort of thing doesn't really matter. She had publicly declared her love for him in Vanity Fair. For me, nothing.

She talks to me briefly. I don't remember whatever it was she says, but I remember the faint sensation of her lips on my cheek, the rough, sweaty hand of the boyfriend shaking mine, and her perfume. Her perfume had a powerful, intoxicating scent. Everything else was void.

Now I'm in the Lower East side, in a dark bar having a drink. Mike meets me there. I see him walk in, vibrant and chock-full of investment banker energy. He was the same way in college.

"You okay buddy?" he asks.

"I'm fine," I lie.

The smile he beams shows me he believes me. I'm dangerous with my emotions. Sometimes I feel I should have played poker, sitting steely-eyed and resolute in my chair, holding my cards in hand as the other players hold their breath wondering what my next move is. The tournament would be held in a place like this; a shadowy bar with mid-90's music blaring from an old radio, the atmosphere saturated with the smell of sweaty men, old wood and whiskey. Mike raises an eyebrow furtively and then smiles once more. I get him a drink. He chats about the usual things; money, work, people being assholes and him starting a gym membership. I nod nonchalantly, staring at the ice cubes melt in my drink.

Two girls bristling with the energy of people in New York for the first time head into the bar and stand beside us. They are from Texas. We initiate a chat and Mike has them laughing in seconds. I already know what will happen. There will be drinks, petulant and anecdote-filled conversations, more drinks, and a foray to an upscale club where we are well known, and then a rendezvous back to Mike's opulent high-rise apartment. They are the two S's, Sarah and Sally. I like their accents. Sally comes closer, and I'm suddenly in pain. She has a sweet, familiar smell; she is wearing the same perfume I smelled on my ex at the show earlier. For a second, I feel the calloused hand of the short, hairy guy on mine, the memory sharp like a pinprick. I give Mike the armband for the after-party.

"I'll meet you there," I say.

He looks surprised, but the ladies don't seem to mind. I feel jittery, regretting the two red bulls I had at the bar. I walk fast and eventually I'm out of the Lower East Side, ambling down quiet residential streets. I emerge near the waterfront. An old Sex and the City joke makes me laugh out loud, even though I'm walking by myself. My laugh sounds hollow, like how I feel. I hear the clicking of heels behind me. Two girls with heavy accents walk by like gazelles, bathed in the amber of streetlights.

"Where are you going?" I ask.

"We are on an adventure," they reply.

"I'll tag along," I say.

I smile, and feel an arm pinch my ribs.

"You're skinny," one of them says.

"Hazards of the occupation," I say with a smile.

I turn the smile on purposefully, diving into my glamour mode; pretending I'm shooting an ad for Gap or Balenciaga. I receive a smile from them both that says good things in subtle ways. They look like twins, attractive with mocha-colored skin, poufy hair and sensuous lips. I already know where they are from, but ask anyway. They tell me they are from Trinidad. I have never been to Trinidad. Perhaps after my next paycheck I may go there. However, flights make me sleepy, so I've stopped flying on planes. Maybe I'll never go to Trinidad.

We walk through a small park, where a homeless lady is reading aloud from a month old newspaper. My fingers tingle slightly. For the last few days that's been happening—little shocks that run up my arm for no reason.

"Hey boy," one of the girls says.

She grabs my arm and points to a street a block away dense with a throng of people. We hear music.

Do you like reggae?" she asks.

I'm not sure anymore, since I stopped listening to music months ago. I hear reggae tracks sometimes when I do runway, but lately I haven't heard the music on the catwalk. I just put on my clothes and strut down the runway, seeing the flashes of strobe lights like tiny white planets in the field of my vision.

"Sure," I reply.

The reggae party is packed wall to wall. The heat from dozens of bodies and the smell of alcohol linger in the air. One of the girls pulls me into the thick of the crowd. I feel her generous body grinding against mine. The friend has disappeared. I dance with her awkwardly. Someone hands me a drink and I sip it. Tequila. The DJ screams something into the microphone. The microphone is bad, and I can't understand what he is saying. The crowd roars in response, and a sea of brown hands go into the air, I raise mine as well, and then a sudden, cold blackness envelops me.

I am swimming in a dark sea with no horizon. My clothes are gone and the water is icy cold. Terror ripples through my body as I feel my body get heavier. I'm sinking into the inky depths and I can't breathe. The city is gone, and all I'm greeted by is the inky blackness and the inability to speak. I scream and scream, but nothing comes out my mouth as I fall deeper and deeper in the invisible ocean.

I open my eyes groggily, and the nausea of returning to the world hits my stomach like a prizefighter's punch. My stomach is empty, but I feel as if I want to throw up. The world returns sense by sense. I hear the hush of voices around me, and I can see pale white light. Maybe I'm dead, I think. Maybe I'm in heaven.

I hear the slightly muted blare of a car horn somewhere, far below me. I don't think they have cabs in heaven. I can feel the rest of myself emerging from my state of unconsciousness. Sheets are on my legs and something is in my arm. Oh god it's a snake! No, not a snake, it's clear and transparent. It is an IV. I'm in the hospital. The white light in my vision shatters into fragments of different sized objects; a chair, the window and an old Zenith television perched on a wall mount. A doctor walks in. He is slim and handsome. He could be an actor.

"How are you feeling?" he asks.

"Fine," I reply.

My voice sounds like a frog with terminal throat cancer.

"You were severely dehydrated and passed out from over exertion. We have you on the IV right now to help you regain some of your bodily fluids, but you'll need to take it easy," he says.

I try to speak, but my throat is parchment. My eyelids are heavy, and my mind screams in alarm. I don't want to sleep. I vaguely remember the girls. He mentions how I got to the hospital and says I'm lucky. I cannot see why. He says a few more things but it becomes a murmur, resonating throughout the small room like a big ripple in a small puddle.

I don't want to sleep, I'm thinking. I don't want to sleep. The doc finishes his spiel.

"A nurse will come by later," he says, turning around.

He pauses at the door.

"Try to get some sleep."

The door closes shut and the temporary drone of outside noise vanishes with a click of the door latch. My arms feel terribly heavy. My vision becomes dark, and slowly I feel myself falling asleep. My mind screams. All I want to be is like the Buddha at the foot of my bed, quiet and ever present. The shapes around me fade into squiggly shadows in front of my eyes, and then everything becomes silent. I'm asleep.

The Scout

The apartment resembled a forgotten tub of bath water, stained, smelly and old. Likewise the kitchen was a menagerie of grime and poor maintenance. Beside the sink, a Tupperware bowl that held ten ounces of water sat idly. In it, a mesh of grayish spaghetti mixed with clumps of brown tuna fish buzzed with the presence of tiny flies. A stale odor floated throughout the expanse of the small Apartment. Not far from it all, in a nearby bedroom, lay Gregory. He shuffled in his bed groaning slightly as sharp bedsprings unceremoniously massaged his back. A small yellow clock on a table beside the bed flashed the current time in bright red letters on its LCD screen. It was three o' clock, and Gregory's flight would be leaving in a few hours. He stood up, feeling a slight draft hit his bare chest. He stretched lightly for a few moments and breathed out heavily.

He looked on the wall closest to his bathroom. On it, was the poster of one of Miami's nicest neighborhoods, a gaudy, sprawling expanse of affluence. In the picture there was a symmetrical image of a street with large houses on either side as far as they eye could see. The grass in the picture was well manicured, the houses spotless, and everything else plastered in pastel. Gregory looked on the picture each day. That's where he wanted to be, eventually. As ratty as his apartment was, Gregory knew he wasn't there completely by choice. Many of his college friends had more lucrative careers like medicine, investment banking or software programming. Gregory had never in his life wanted to be a doctor. In fact, he didn't want to be any of the traditionally accepted 'good' jobs like a doctor, lawyer, architect or an engineer. He wanted something with a touch of difference, a break from the mold of the political DC atmosphere he grew up in. He wanted the kind of career people hear about and are immediately fascinated by. This apartment was temporary—as temporary as three years paying the rent can be. Gregory grew up in a less than glamorous section of Washington D.C as a kid—an edgy Suburb in South

East. After four blurry years of college and traipsing about town as a bartender for another three and a half years, he found his calling far away from home. Gregory Peck, or Peck as his friends always called him, worked for a large real estate firm in Miami.

The first day he worked there, one sentence from his then-new boss captured the theme of his journey to date: "Welcome to *that* place *you* need to be Gregory." The sentence sounded weird to him now, but at the time had helped Gregory to feel special. The building was a sprawling office tucked away in South Beach, that microcosm of narcissism where everyone was a chiseled, walking mannequin. The company had done well in Miami, getting contracts for major apartment developments, governments building developments and hotels. Once his boss got a taste for the hotel business he expanded his portfolio, seeking what he termed 'exotic real estate'. For him, the boss man, real estate, good or bad was like a piece of coal; he would market it, hype it up, promote like mad and blow away the competition. When the dust cleared, there was a diamond in its place.

It was a Tuesday, and Gregory was happy to be leaving Miami. Beside his foot, a roach the size of an Oreo cookie announced its presence as it walked slowly into the room from a crack in the wall. Its feelers twitched for a few seconds as it searched for food. Apparently unimpressed, it returned slowly to its dark confines in the wall. The presence of this vermin in his living space had long stopped bothering Gregory. His days were twelve hours long and he saw everything through jaded eyes at night, usually with a bottle of whiskey in hand. But he had worked hard, and this new assignment could change everything. If all went well, he could leave this apartment within a month, maybe two. Then he would be closer to his slice of the big pie; maybe closer to having his own pastel house with the nice, trimmed lawn. He strolled into the bathroom and looked into the mirror. It was spotted with gray stains and had a hairline crack that ran from the top to the middle of the mirror. He forced himself to smile back at his tired face. At least his teeth were white, he thought with a chuckle.

"I love Jamaica," the boss had said randomly to him one day.

That day, they were taking a walk on the beach, outside the office. The boss did that on occasion with random employees; he'd tap them on the shoulder and gesture to the back entrance and discuss business ideas or just life while walking on the beach.

"I want to make a huge, beautiful mountain lodge. Something not near the cities, heck, I want something you have to *want* to go to. I want somewhere up in the hills you see?"

At this point he gestured with his cane towards the sky, as if pointing towards hills that had mysteriously popped up out of the Miami coastline overnight. The old guy was a wealthy landowner from Texas who came to Miami for its usual cocktail of women, drugs and the fast life. Even though he was in his sixties, he fit the classic Miami profile well with a healthy cosmetic tan, dressed in a sky blue linen shirt, loose-fitting pants and dark leather Birkenstocks.

"I want you to scout this for me Greg. Make it beautiful and I'll make it worth your while."

Gregory's had felt his head swell with anticipation in that moment. The boss did the same thing with another fellow a few months back, a sharp-witted employee name Kevin. For Kevin, it ended up being a fifty thousand dollar payday after he successfully found a location somewhere in Peru. Kevin was a scout.

In the office there were about twenty-five employees, with three of those being seasoned scouts. The scouts were part architect, part businessman, and part artist. The boss would have the vision; the scout would work to make it real. After the boss laid out his grandiose plan to have the latest villa or mountain resort, the scout would begin the process of vetting the location. There were many ways to get something like this done of course, but the boss loved sending someone who didn't know the territory there to see what they could discover. If they were successful, they'd get a massive bonus. Most people in the office just thought it was one of those quirky millionaire habits, like spelunking or buying Da-Hong Pao tea. It took a few years for people to be considered a scout, based on criteria that only the boss seemed to be aware of. Gregory was in year number three. He had started out collecting mail and grabbing coffee, but had learned from dog duty many of the ins and outs of real estate acquisition, property evaluations and had secured a few small projects for the office to sink their teeth into. Whatever the boss wanted in Jamaica, he would make it happen.

His things were already packed in a small Samsonite suitcase. It had an assortment of bare essentials; a bundle of clothes, and male toiletries. It was a quiet drive to the airport, and Gregory drifted in and out of sleep, seeing the rolling clouds and the blue sky of the Miami landscape in flashes of black and blue through the cab window. He felt a sudden jerk, and woke up. They had arrived at the Miami International Airport. Gregory coasted through the large walkways and security checkpoints, reaching his terminal with time to spare and waited. An hour and a half later, he was in Jamaica.

This was his second time to the beautiful island. When he was seven he came with his family to a resort for a few days. Only one memory remained from that trip up by the North Coast. There was a nude beach that he snuck onto, and found himself staring at a host of fat, sun burnt men walking around without a care in the world, penises wiggling like sticks of rubber as they walked. Women were there too, sitting with it all bared for anyone to see on the beach, slathering sunburned with suntan lotion or walking around in groups. It was a scary, frightening thing for Gregory to see, (possibly because all these people were extremely fat), but the memory was as clear as a tape recording. Now there would be no beaches, just countryside.

The boss was interested in some property in the mountains near to Ocho Rios. When he was on the plane, Gregory had flipped through a book with a bit of information on the island. The island had fourteen parishes, divided into three counties, Cornwall, Middlesex and Surrey. He felt that one place in particular; St. Ann might be worth checking out first. This was the parish where the popular tourist town of Ocho Rios was located. A side note in the guidebook said that locals called it *"Ochi"*. Eight rivers ran through the parish, hence the name *a la* espanol.

A bus picked him up to carry him to a lodge near the property. The drive was long, because they had to drive from Montego Bay to Ocho Rios. The scenery mesmerized Gregory. Lush vegetation rolled over the hills like a herd of wildebeest. Tall green grass stretched for miles, sitting on plains filled with ancient trees and hidden groves. Houses and businesses appeared to be embedded into the countryside, quite like they had started out as seeds of concrete and steel and bloomed into houses. The air was heavy with moisture and the scent of plants and fruit trees. He could see the hills his boss had spoken about, staring at him like green giants having a quiet conversation in the calm atmosphere of the afternoon. A small road caught his eye. It led into a quiet-looking enclave of trees, which expanded into a large hillside.

"Can we turn around please?" Gregory said to the driver.

They turned around and pulled onto the small road. Inside Gregory something tingled, the same instinct that had helped him find a few dilapidated apartments in Miami that turned out to be a goldmine for the development company. He took out a few green bills and paid the driver, whose name was Roy, and stepped out.

"Where you going? You not going to the hotel?" Roy said.

Gregory had no real idea. All he knew was that the boss wanted him to try and find some suitable hilly areas. Ocho Rios was an extremely popular tourist town. A super-inclusive lodge only a few miles away just might work.

"Is there anywhere I can stay around here, like a small hotel or something?" Gregory asked.

Roy smirked, as if saying to himself *this foreigner.*

"There is a place just up the road. You sure you don't want to go into town, into Ochi?" he asked.

"No thanks," Gregory replied.

They were on a small trail just off the main road. A slight wind rustled in the bushes, and there were several trees so large their branches hung over most of the roadway. Little pebbles and stones adorned the sides of the roads like fallen confetti. There were no sidewalks, just grooves in the sides of the road, long smears of brown. Somewhere, a goat yelped and Gregory felt the thick countryside aroma waft into his nose. He liked the smell, a perfect blend of rustic and pungent. This was the kind of place to wake up in the morning, maybe go for a run or have breakfast on an elegant patio. He stepped back into the small bus and they drove up the road for a few more minutes. The further they drove there were less traces of man's presence. The roads were rougher and more undulating, the trees bigger and more menacing, the grass tall and untrained. The bus came to a stop. Roy pointed to a barely discernible path that led into the bushes.

"That's you right there," Roy said.

For the duration of the journey thus far, Roy had been quite pleasant, but there was no smile on his face now.

"Ask for Mr. Edwards and he will set you up with a room," he said quietly.

"Thanks Roy," Gregory said as he stepped out with his suitcase.

He took out another twenty-dollar bill to hand to Roy, but the bus was already driving away, it's engine an alien scream in the quiet countryside. Gregory pulled a zip on his suitcase, revealing a pair of straps like those you see on any kid's backpack. He slipped it on and headed towards the path. The grass was *very* high, well over six feet, and a fog of silence hung heavily over the area, save the sound of his shoes hitting the cracked earth with each step. Many parts of the path hadn't been used in sometime, and wild, itchy grass grew in large uneven patches, many of which Gregory had to step directly through. The heat had risen, and his shirt stuck to his skin.

To his left, a dark blur slipped in between stalks of grass followed by a loud crunching noise. Startled, Gregory looked up the path. No more than four feet away from him stood a man. His skin was as dark as night and his eyes were perfectly white. His head had soft, matted hair that grew into a series of unruly locks. The man appeared timeless. There were no wrinkles on his face, but he projected an aura of terrifying, secret knowledge. Gregory was momentarily transfixed. The man stood there for several pregnant seconds, not appearing to notice that Gregory was staring at him.

"Uh-can you tell me where the lodge is?" Gregory said.

The man did not speak. When he did, his accent was rough, and heavily inflected.

"*Yuh nuh wah fi go deh,*" he said.

The voice was thunderously deep and came from multiple directions in a chorus. A strange feeling crept up Gregory's spine.

"Excuse me?" Gregory asked.

The thick heat had faded somehow. Did it feel—cold? The man stared at him directly through those piercing white eyes.

"*Suku Yaaaa,*" he said.

The sound of the word struck Gregory like a splash of frigid water. Whatever it meant spoke of something ancient and terrible, from a time of pain and darkness. A soft wind blew between the high stalks and behind him, something rustled. He looked back, seeing nothing. When he turned around, the man was gone. All was hot and quiet again. Gregory stood with his hands on his side, trying to make sense of it all. Then he heard a voice.

"Hey you!" a voice said.

Gregory tensed as a man appeared from a bend in the path. He wore old blue dungarees and a sun-faded Polo shirt. The man was tall and bronzed. He had a straight nose bridge but his nose was wide, his eyes had a hint of blue in them and his hair, though cut short, was very curly. Gregory guessed he was of mixed ethnicity. Even his accent sounded different from Roy's. Still Jamaican, but different somehow.

"I'm Mr. Edwards, but you can call me Eddie," he said.

He beamed a friendly smile, and for a moment, Gregory almost forgot about the mysterious man.

"What is *Sookoo yaa?*" Gregory said.

Mr. Edwards smile faded like fresh ink washing off a smooth surface. He had seen fear earlier in Roy's eyes, but Mr. Edwards had a darker, quieter expression on his face. He looked at Gregory for a few seconds without responding, then smiled again, with even more brilliance.

"Oh, that's nothing man. Local stuff. So what brings you here?"

They started walking up the path, which opened into a wide field after a few meters. A hundred or so yards away was a small house, with a large ancient SUV in the driveway. Behind the house, the hill continued upwards, blanketed in unusual darkness even though it was still the middle of the day. They reached the house and sat on two chairs outside on the verandah. Gregory explained to him his plans for the lodge and his scouting tasks. With every mention of the word "investment" or "financing" Mr. Edwards eye's widened. After five minutes, it was like they were best friends.

"I have a cabin up at the top of the hill that you can stay in while you try and figure out if this place is for you, but I guarantee it is."

Mr. Edwards grabbed a beer from his fridge and offered it to Gregory. He politely declined and took a soda instead. They left the house and started walking up the hillside. The earth was looser going up this path, and the thick gnarled roots of trees crisscrossed like veins in the brown soil.

"Now at the top here," Mr. Edwards said. "You have to be careful, because there is a steep drop over there."

He pointed towards a slope that was filled with jagged rocks. They walked for another minute and Gregory saw the cabin. It was small and rugged, painted in an off-white color. Cracks ran through the length of the house, and inside was dark and quiet.

"So you see the lights work, and there's the kitchen and the bedroom. I'll have Miss P bring some food up for you, but don't worry about paying, you can stay for free until you make your decision about the property."

Mr. Edward's voice had gained a high pitch of confidence, as if Gregory had offered him to buy the land already.

"In here," he pointed towards the kitchen. "We have a few useful things. Sometimes a stray goat or small animal might come inside and you just rush it out with any of these." He opened a small cabinet showing an assortment of gardening tools.

"I used to keep a shotgun in here somewhere, but I haven't seen it in a while. You won't need that anyways," he chuckled.

"I wouldn't recommend you come down the hill at night unless it's absolutely necessary. But if you really need something, walk down the path and knock on my door. Just be careful at nighttime and use this."

He took up a massive, ancient flashlight and rested it on the counter. He turned it on and off a few times to make sure the battery was working. After he left, Gregory felt the toll of his traveling hit him at once. He rested his bag near a desk that was rotting with age and flopped onto the bed. Gregory thought for a moment about the white eyes of the man he saw on the path then closed his eyes. It was hot and his shirt was still wet from the heat, but he fell quickly asleep.

****

A loud rapping noise made Gregory jump up. Briefly, he felt disoriented, forgetting where he was. It was evening now, still hot but the sky was no longer bright outside. The rapping noise came again. It was the door. Shuffling out of bed and checking his breath—an old childhood habit, he opened the door. A short, heavyset lady was standing there. She was broad and dark-skinned bursting with the strength of a woman used to a life in the hills. She held a tray in her hands.

"Mr. Edward said I was to give this to you," she said in a husky voice.

Whatever it was, it smelled delicious.

"Thank you miss?"

"Miss P."

She turned to walk away, and Gregory suddenly had a flashback of the man on the path; cool, dark, ancient. He rested the tray on a small table on the patio of the cabin.

"Uh, Miss P?" he said.

She turned and looked at him. In the fading light, the purple-blue of the evening sky rippled off her dark skin.

"I saw this man earlier today, I didn't know who he was, but he said something about *Sookoo Yaa?*"

At the mention of the word, Miss P's eyes widened slightly, but she didn't register the same fear as Roy or Mr. Edward's odd expression. She simply stood there, in the gloom for a quiet moment.

"Enjoy your dinner," she said.

She disappeared down the path as easily as a shadow in a dark room. Gregory rubbed his temples for a second. Miami felt curiously distant, like a dot of light in the sky. He sat on one of the patio chairs and dug into the meal Miss P had made for him. It was the most delicious food he had ever tasted. There were soft yellow yams, salted fish, firm gray bananas and a few other delicacies he couldn't name. It was filling, and after he finished Gregory sat there for a while, listening to the soft noise of the countryside.

Then a sound wafted through the air, soft but familiar. It was the sound of jingling of chains. He opened his eyes with a start, and stood up. The noise echoed again, somewhere far-off.

Clink. Clink. Clink.

Gregory paid it no mind, casually watching the evening drift away. The purple-blue light soon faded, and the hillside evanesced into a sheet of shadow. Save the chirping of a few scattered crickets, the night was still. Gregory walked inside with his tray in hand, and put his plate in the sink. The soda Mr. Edwards gave him earlier was still on the small, smelly desk beside his bed. He grabbed it and popped the cap open. He took a few sips, feeling the bubbles caress the insides of his throat. A loud *Clap!* sounded throughout the cabin, causing him to nearly fall off the bed. The front door shook angrily and there was another *Clap!* Gregory paused for a few moments, startled. Maybe it is Miss P, he thought. He opened the door and took a step outside the doorway.

Gregory paused in the darkness. Around him, the air tickled his forearms in a hedgy fog of sprinkled darts. He let out a fuzzy gray breath, astonished by the snakelike wisps of cold condensed air swirling in front of his eyes. This moment of fascination would not last. In front of him, in the gloom of the night, the forest screamed. Giant bushes fell to the earth, as if cut from an invisible blade, and clods of dust exploded in bursts all around him. The patio shook with an unseen force— and a moaning wind from the depths of some dead man's nightmare roared. A hissing noise made Gregory jump in fright and he almost laughed when he realized he had dropped his soda. Then *it* came.

Gregory was paralyzed by the sound heavy, wet sound of enormous of footsteps coming towards him. He spun around, not wanting to see whatever *it* was. He clutched the door handle shakily, hearing a snarl behind him. His heart was in his throat. The footsteps were coming. The door opened easily— Gregory smashed his knee on the doorway in the process—

and fell inside. Behind him a large red eye the size of a grapefruit passed by, silhouetted by an enormous black shape. Still holding his right knee, he kicked the door shut with his boot heel. Catching his breath, he listened.

Silence coated the cabin. There was no longer that intense, wailing wind. At first it had sounded like a car engine, but became a cacophony of animal sounds meshed together, singing in a horrific orchestra. All Gregory could hear were his own breaths, and the thumping of his heart. He got up and ran into the center of the main room. The cabin had only three rooms; a small living room area, a kitchen and a small bedroom. In the kitchen there was a closet with a few utilities and cleaning supplies. Gregory took a hesitant glance through the living room window. His eyes were met with darkness. There was no blur of motion, no large red eye. Gregory wondered if he had really seen it, if the wind and the noise were all some strange reaction to Miss P's meal. He stepped into the kitchen warily, and reached into the utility cabinet. He bent down to grab a rake, and a small swirl of dust hit the air with a *poof*. Gregory let out a muffled moan. It was true! The noise, that eye, that thing. He grabbed the large flashlight and the rake. The caretaker had told him there was a shotgun in here, but where? Whatever that thing, that shape was couldn't be stopped with just a rake could it? His knee was tingling with pain, and a dark red smear stained his pants at the knee. He looked through the kitchen window again unable to see anything in the pitch. There was no sound, no wind rustling in the trees. No more crickets. Not even the tips of the mountains which were visible just minutes ago. They were all gone. A laugh sounded directly behind him.

"Jesus Christ!" Gregory exclaimed with a swing of the rake.

The long garden tool smashed into a dishwashing tray packed with knives and old plates. They fell to the ground with a ferocious clatter, sending bits of ceramic flying. The pieces hit the wall and then settled while Gregory stood there, holding the rake at the invisible laughing man. The laugh came again, from a different part of the cabin, the bedroom. It was a boyish laugh, sweet and tinkling. He instinctively looked out the window again, but it seemed even darker than before out there, as if nothing had ever existed in that void. Another laugh came from the bedroom. He gripped the rake with both hands, and started towards the bedroom.

The crunch of his boot on a piece of broke plate made him curse loudly. He took a breath and made a few authoritative steps towards the bedroom. He pushed the door open with the handle of the rake. A slight chuckle echoed below him somewhere. The bed—yes, it was coming from the bed. No, under the bed. The chuckle swelled into that boyish laugh again, and shut off abruptly in mid laugh, like someone hanging up a phone. Gregory felt a drop of sweat hang idly on the tip of his nose, then fall to the ground. Whatever it was that was happening here, Gregory couldn't understand it. He was a reasonable man, a practical man. Sure he'd done some drugs in his time but—then it came again. The laugh was deep this time, like a voice recording at half-speed. It sounded harsh, and demonic. The laugh spread from under the bed to the entire room, booming through cracks in the wall. Gregory leapt back in fright, cursing to himself. The laughing boy, or rather, the thing, was taunting him. He didn't want to go back outside. *It* was out there. That shape, that blur.

"Gregory," the voice chanted. "*Greeeeeggoorriiie.*"

The voice reached a higher and higher pitch, till Gregory found himself with both hands on his ears. The rake and flashlight were rattling on the floor. The whole house was unhinged by the shrill noise. A window behind him shattered and in the kitchen the utensils on the floor clinked and clanked, hopping in a frenzy. Something wet was on Gregory's palms, and he realized it was blood from his ears. He began to scream, and then the noise stopped. Where the window was broken, it had let in an icy wind. It swirled in a lecherous dance around Gregory, touching his neck and hands with tiny, frozen fingers. That was the last straw.

He grabbed the rake and light once more and rushed towards the door, opening it tentatively. He stepped onto the patio. The temperature was normal out here, at least for the moment. He squinted to see beyond the dim glow cast by the cabin's modest lighting. The small trees he had seen earlier that day near the path were crushed, torn asunder by whatever had floated by with the giant red eye. The soda bottle was still where he left it, resting in a small red-orange pool of liquid. He hesitated in the face of the endless black. Goosebumps prickled Gregory's flesh as he thought of those invisible fingers touching his skin again. He took a step outside the door, and then *it* came.

Whatever it was, it was huge—twice the size of a small car. The gigantic form floated past noiselessly, hovering a few inches from the ground. Thin tendrils of cold fumes came from unseen holes in its body. The shape stopped and faced him. Two eyes popped dramatically out of the black mass; large red orbs, with tiny black irises. The icy wind was back. Gregory wanted to move, but he couldn't, and let out a tiny yelp as his cold shirt touched his back, mimicking the feel of a small hand. The shape jiggled before him, shifting in and out like a blur of guts and bone, until the metamorphosis stopped. In front of him was a bull, larger than any Gregory had ever seen. Cold vapor streamed from its nostrils and its face was covered in deep, thickly grooved scars. An odor worse than a gravedigger's nightmare hit him dead in the face. The animal was at least nine feet high, and stared quietly at Gregory. Tiny worms were crawling in and out of the grooves in its face. Maggots.

The howling wind came again, swishing and tearing things in its path. The patio shook and Gregory fell heavily to his knees. Sparks of pain shot up his thigh. The howling originated from the beast. Its mouth wasn't open, but the sound was coming directly from it. Its eyes, bubbling red and black, screamed with madness, pain and anger. The howling became a roar, and this time the creature opened its mouth, spreading its fetid odor in a wet blanket. The creature rushed forward, a mass of stink and death. Its horns were at least four feet long, and Gregory could already imagine the wet, crushed sound of his chest as he was gored. The creature lunged, and Gregory braced for impact. The icy tip of one of the creature's horns pierced his chest slightly, the sensation akin to being stung by a giant bee. He screamed and clutched himself as the beast collapsed in front of him, melting into a large black puddle. The ebon liquid swished violently in a serpent like motion and shot away at incredible speed into the hillside. Again, the wind died, and there was no noise. Gregory got up and sprinted towards the small path that led off the small hill the cabin rested atop. His mind ran on what Mr. Edwards had said earlier.

I wouldn't recommend taking the path at night, unless it's absolutely necessary.

"It is absolutely goddamn necessary!" Gregory heard himself shout.

His knee was beginning to feel swollen and tight, and with each pump of his legs through the darkness and the bush, it worsened. The roar sounded behind him again, farther away but not very far. Gregory stopped briefly, and realized only a foot in front of him, was the steep drop onto the hillside. The very hillside Mr. Edwards had spoken about. A sick feeling hit his stomach as he saw himself on those rocks, with his head split open and grey matter leaking onto the healthy mountain soil. He glanced at the ground, seeing the familiar thinning of the grass and evidence of trimming and started running again. He wheezed, feeling his chest tight with fatigue. The night air wasn't cold, but it was getting cooler. That meant *it* was closer. The bushes rustled again, only a few feet away this time. The dead cow-thing was coming, and for a moment Gregory could smell it, maggots and all. His foot hit a rogue tree root and he felt himself briefly weightless. Then he impacted heavily on the ground, and something tore at his side. Groaning in pain he heard the sound that was a distant echo earlier that evening.

Clink…Clink.

The clinking noise of a thousand chains. Gregory got up and felt a hot wave of pain on his left side. Maybe he had bruised a rib, or worse. Limping and holding his side he made his way down the steep enclave with the thick tree roots. With every other step, he stubbed his feet on exposed roots, or raked his hands on low hanging tree branches. He came to a small clearing and in the distance he could see the faint glow of Mr. Edwards' house. Then the roar came again. The powerful, overwhelming stench dropped on him in a dense cloud. The beast was behind him, smashing everything in its wake. Gregory sprinted like he never had before. The grass shook and the earth rumbled. Only twenty yards or so would save him from the frightening clutches of the night and certain death by the creature from hell. He ran, feeling the tips of the wind's cold fingers scratch his neck. He leapt onto the patio of Mr. Edward's house and rapped furiously on the door.

"Let me in!" Gregory screamed. "Mr. Edwards!"

Gregory pounded the door until he felt himself pounding air, then being lifted by a set of powerful hands. He was righted onto his feet, which sent more bullets of pain through his body, and he saw who was holding him. It was Miss P.

"What was that?" he said.

His voice was brittle.

"It is torture," Miss P said.

"Torture? What the hell is that supposed to mean?" Gregory asked.

"It is death, a symbol from the past of ills and evils done wrong. It is an amalgam of evil, something from the depth. From the depth."

The depth.

He groaned, the pain in his side a welder's flame near his ribs. With each breath, something went *plut* in his side. His vision swam in between white and red, and Miss P's face became a fuzzy image. She continued speaking, but Gregory could no longer hear her. Her voice sounded like a harmonic grouping of several things, man and animal alike. In front of his eyes, she rippled, changing her very body. She squatted on the ground and changed into a small goat, bleating loudly. The goat ran around in circles for a moment, then it looked straight at Gregory and its eyes grew to three times their size, popping out of their sockets, shooting a slimy liquid onto Gregory's hands. The eyes combusted and he could see flames shooting through the eye sockets. The innards of the goat's eyes were burning, dripping red liquid onto the ground and the creature exploded in a ball of fire. He gagged as the smell of burning, spoiled meat filled the air. The flames spread into two and Gregory saw the shape of the man he had seen earlier, by the path, then he saw Miss P's shape reform, then the massive creature returned. It grew so large that the supporting fence that was constructed around the base of the patio shattered. It roared again, loudly with a voice from the pits of hell. A hoof the size of a small person threatened to squash Gregory and he ran to the side as it almost stepped on him. Cursing himself, he wished he had never taken this assignment. He heard a beeping noise behind him. He clutched his face, half expecting the massive beast to shoot him with a ray of fire, but it was Mr. Edwards in his jeep. He was waving hurriedly at him. Gregory hopped in, feeling his broken rib move upward as he sat in the seat. He screamed in pain and all went black.

****

The rough shaking of the car woke Gregory up. How long had he blacked out? Not long he reasoned, the car had just exited the grass path to the country road. A friendlier wind caressed Gregory's face as the large jeep drove quickly in the nighttime darkness. Mr. Edwards had that look of fear in his eyes again. He pulled over to the side of the road by a clear patch of road with no trees. Bullets of sweat dotted Gregory's forehead, the pain beyond the range of his mind.

"What happened there?" Gregory said groggily.

Mr. Edwards didn't answer. He was looking up at the night sky. The moon, full, naked and obvious shone over them. The moonlight hit Mr. Edwards face, turning it into a bright, white mask.

"I feel like hell," Gregory said.

Mr. Edwards did not reply, as he was still looking at the moon. Then Gregory gasped, once his eyes fell onto the steering wheel. Mr. Edwards's hands were large, distended and furry with long black nails each like a short blade protruding from each fingertip. Mr. Edwards turned his face to Gregory and smiled. A smile of sharp, brilliantly white teeth.

"*Suku Yaaaaa*," he said.

Femme Fatale

It was sometime in March, maybe a year ago now that we met, when I was doing a week of training with my fellow English teachers. We were a somewhat motley crew of folks, hailing from Canada, the U.S, Jamaica, England and Australia. Like most of the folks there, I knew nothing about Japan except what I'd read in magazines or seen in little vignettes in the media over the years. I, of course did not believe that an entire culture would only be fascinated with robots or Samurai and did not enter the country with those expectations. But being in a new culture carried with it a lot of heavy weight and one could see that effect on the trainees, plucked from all over the globe, battle scarred from lengthy international travel, thrust immediately into a vigorous weeklong training. We were all in our twenties I think, and it didn't take long for that restless pool of hormones and testosterone to brave the unknown streets of this new city in a good old-fashioned drink up. After a day of training, maybe around Wednesday, we roamed in an innocent mob to a nearby bar. It was a bar packed with Japan-savvy foreigners, and the discovery of such a bar ignited the flames of the trainees. Especially after discovering that 7-11s sold a bonanza of cheap drinks, some of the more extroverted trainees would soon have parties in their hotel rooms and there would be whispers of hookups and late night madness happening till the early hours. As much as I liked to party, I was still suffering terribly from jet lag. It had been hitting me all week and left me waking up at odd hours, unsure of the time and occasionally, very thirsty. A frequent disorientation would hit me in waves, the air around me a wet blanket. In these moments I felt my stomach curdle, and my throat fill with liquid, but I never threw up. It was all phantom, all part of the adjustment process. Thankfully none of these ill spells affected me during training, more so during the mornings or evenings.

During this time I went out almost every night, exploring the city. I didn't ever like to sleep too much in a new place because I hated losing my sense of direction day after day. I settled on three places as my common cardinal points. There was the No Name bar, a haven for foreigners, Daichi dori, a sort of hip strip with a collection of restaurants, bars and shopping stores and of course, the hotel where I was staying. One of the three points, The No Name bar, is where I met Femme Fatale.

She was one of a host of revolving characters I met during this time, including a fellow called Pepsi Boy, a giant hawk-nosed man known as Texas (even though he is Turkish) and a mysterious Japanese fellow who always wore giant UFO pants that called himself Five. It wasn't any sort of exceptional meeting, that first time. I sat with a handful of my colleagues, raving about the cultural impact of the movie *Tron* versus *Blade Runner.* The conversation was getting pretty heated, because I thought Blade Runner was obviously more culturally relevant, but Pepsi Boy vehemently disagreed with me. It was around this time, Femme Fatale came up to me, oblivious to our loud ravings and rested one of her small hands on my chest.

"I don't date sexy men," she said to me assertively, before walking away.

What she meant by that was lost on me, in this new, fuzzy world of jet lag and all day training sessions. In twenty-five years the only women who had ever called me handsome were limited to my mother and a handful of aunts. I called her Femme Fatale because I grew up watching this old TV show, good at the time but probably deplorable now, called *La Femme Nikita,* about a prototypically blonde super spy who kicked ass and took names. I wouldn't say she was the splitting image of the actress, but that's the first thing that popped into my mind when I met her, and it stuck. I would learn in short order she was notorious for saying random things, prone to unusual mood swings and could outdrink any man or woman within a hundred mile radius. As a Jamaican I did not know many Russians, and she was one of the handful I had encountered in my life thus far. I saw her pretty much every night I went out during this initial phase of my arrival and we'd sometimes share drinks but always with a group, ranting and raving until the early hours.

I realized at this time Japan was a complete illusion for us, the trainees. None of us had apartments, bank accounts or cell phones yet. Having a hotel room of our own for a week removed us all from the quickly approaching demands of true adult responsibility. I was quite determined to do well, and put a lot of effort into my training exercises and mock teaching classes during the days. Apparently, I was good at the *big voice,* which commanded a lot of attention in a classroom, especially the rowdy ones. I was warned that all the kids weren't as cute and docile as people thought, prone to the usual high school fare of fistfights and acts of teenage rebellion. One weekend after training had ended, a horde of the trainees, stumbled into the hotel lobby, drunk and loud, singing pop songs. I witnessed this with a bemused look at the time, assuming it was the pressure of the week that had caused this behavior to emerge. I was wrong. I quickly discovered, that Japan is quite the drinking country.

Only in Japan had I ever seen piles of unusually attractive women lying outside a club in a heap, completely drunk, unable to move. It was also the first place I had consistently seen men trying to light each others crotches on fire, strangers repeatedly try and grab my dick for kicks and see people passed out the street with such frequency that it was considered normal. I saw men in three thousand dollar suits sprawled out and asleep on the sidewalk, and extremely well-dressed women lying face down on the pavement; lifeless dolls. I made it a habit (If I was not also drunk and struggling to get home) to occasionally take pictures of these folk. At first it was for voyeuristic posterity, but then I wondered, what if these people disappeared? Maybe I could volunteer some information, I dunno. But Japan is a place where I, the foreigner followed two rules: *Do not touch. Do not stare.*

My first major exposure to this phenomenon was at work event of all places. It was called a *Bonenkai,* some kind of end of year party. I was a mess when I arrived because I couldn't find the venue, which was somewhere just out of town. I'd only been in the country for two weeks at that point, and hadn't figured out how to properly navigate the Japanese streets, or take trains yet. I was panicked because in training I'd heard over and over *don't EVER be late*.

Despite my tardiness, once I arrived I was greeted warmly by a member of the school staff and ushered into a simple conference room. Inside were about one hundred people, a mixture of teachers and parents all seated at tables low to the ground. The Vice principal, who up to that point I had never seen smile and barley said a word to me (or anyone) since I started teaching at the school bounced over to me.

"HALLO! HOW ARE YOU?" he screamed at me.

For a moment, I was shocked, remembering the two rules of my training that our coach had emphasized. *No touching, No staring*. Now here I was, with the Vice principal with his meaty arm around my shoulder.

"GOOD TO SEE YOU. COME, COME!" he bellowed, gesturing at an empty seat by one of the tables.

The night would be one of legend. Since drinking is such a part of the culture in Japan, we had an entire presentation on drinking etiquette during our training week. One thing to note was that people could take offense if they poured you a drink and you did not accept it. Secondly, as a courtesy, should you have an empty glass in your hand in a social gathering, someone will probably refill it for you. Thirdly, you might be expected to go 'toe to toe' with your Japanese colleagues, as it is a form of bonding, especially in a business setting. As I sat beside the Vice Principal to my left and the head of the English department to my right, some of the locals, mothers of students I would be teaching became quite enamored with me, ensuring my glass was not empty the entire evening. That night I would set a record, having drunk twenty-eight beers.

The following Monday when I arrived to work, there was no indication the raucous staff party had ever happened. There was no mention of me badly trying to sing along with a popular Japanese song with the staff or the school principal confessing to me he loved me at the train station before I went home. Much later, I learned the term *Bonenkai* meant literally, 'forget the year' and it made much more sense why people went bananas with the drinking and crazy behavior.

Then there was my injury that first week. This was not good due to the fact that it took around a week to get signed up for health insurance and all that good stuff and we were repeatedly warned, *do not get injured.* The situation happened after coming back to the hotel from a night out in one of the simplest situations one can imagine, taking a picture. The jacket I wore then had an interesting design. It was a well-tailored coat with a thin hoodie sewn in the fabric. The head of the hood could be adjusted by pulling two elastic strings with small black knobs on the end of the string. When I raised my camera up to take a picture (in the elevator of all places), one of those knobs got caught in my camera strap, stretched the string to its full length, which wound up and released, whipping back to its point of origin, slapping me in my left eye at full throttle. My eye stung with pain in the moment, but it didn't last more than a few minutes. I was fine for the next day or two, able to finish my training with no issues. It was three days later, one day after moving into my apartment that things changed.

Light stung my eyes like needles with the slightest movement of my eyelids. My room was pitch black, save the dim light of my laptop's screensaver, which might as well have been the sun in the room. I gritted my teeth and went under the covers, but light slithered under there as well and stung my eyes again with such force I had to cover both eyes with my left hand, while groping around for the laptop to close it. The voice of my cherubic trainer echoed in my mind: *Remember guys don't get injured!* I almost laughed. This wasn't a split lip or a sprained ankle. I barley knew where I lived and didn't even have a cell phone. After lying down for an hour I got up, and navigated towards the blinds that faced a large window by my very small verandah, where I had a drying pole for laundry.

My eyes were clenched as tightly as I could make them, and when I opened the blinds, everything went white despite my shut eyelids and I staggered back, the pain like pokers digging into my retinas. Panicking, I tried to think clearly. Whatever was happening might be quite serious and I certainly didn't want to go blind through ignorance. Obviously I needed to see a doctor but not only did I have no phone to call anyone, I couldn't use the laptop to send an e-mail *and* I didn't exactly remember how to navigate the streets back to my hotel. I used one of my work ties, a black one, to cover my eyes. A few throbbing moments later I saw that it was the left eye, the one that got hit a few days ago that screamed in agony the most (although the right eye was screaming pretty loudly too). I wrapped the tie tight around both eyes, with just enough give for the right eye, which still hurt like hell but allowed me to see blurry images in a squint.

I walked outside, somehow making it to a convenience store a few blocks away where I bought a pair of sunglasses for a thousand yen. I slipped them on, and I had temporary relief. The light still hurt immensely, and I still wore a tie over the left eye. I took long deep breaths and tried to remember where the hotel was. With my eyes squinted I could not look up at street signs or peer down roads and feared permanently damaging my eyes if they were to hit direct sunlight. My frequent early forays into the city had helped me with my sense of direction and I eventually made it to the hotel and entered the lobby, where finally I got some assistance.

For the rest of the day I operated like this, wearing the glasses indoors and out. My eyes felt less stressed and the shots of pain weren't as significant. This lead me to think my condition was improving, but I was wrong. The next day, it was worse. I could barely get out of bed from the pain and now had extreme concerns about permanent eye damage. Fortunately, my company had arranged for me to meet with what is called an I.C. (International Correspondent). Today she was helping me out with the visit to the doctor, but would eventually help me to get some furniture for my place and a cell phone. She drove, so at the very least I was able to hide from the growling sun behind tinted glass window for a while. When we reached the doctor's office and exited the car, the pain from the light hitting my eyes was so bad I had to navigate my way inside in slow steps, following the soles of her feet until we entered the doctor's office. Today, my eye armour was a sleep mask and my pair of dark glasses on top of those. I could sense the presence of many people around me, but the darkness drew me into deep thought between time and space. For the last two days I had been the dark, a prisoner of light.

Then, I heard my name. I expected My I.C. Miss Nakamura, to help me, but had she excused herself to go to the bathroom just moments before they called my name. I squinted in bursts of pain as a tall, balding man in a white doctor's coat barked instructions at me. I don't understand a word of what he is saying, but from his gestures I think he is telling me to look forward and tell him what I can see. I have taken my sleep mask and glasses off, but have my eyes clenched tight and try I explain to him in whatever Japanese I know that I cannot open my eyes. He let out a huff, like a fat dog flopping on a couch and motioned for me to go back into the waiting room. Miss Nakamura hadn't returned yet, and I slipped the eye patch back on, and fell into darkness again for a while. Eventually, miss Nakamura returned and we went to see the doctor. He was a different fellow from the first person I saw. This person was a man with short graying hair and kind eyes. We all sat in a dimly lit room and I was guided to sit in front of a giant machine. He rested my jaw gently on a metal plate protruding from the device and told me to open my eyes. I did so, quite surprised that I did not experience with my eyes open this time. The device flashed blue, yellow and read beams of light into my eyes.

"Mae o mitte kudasai," (look forward) he said.

"Hidari to ue mitte kudaisa," (up and left) he said.

He repeated the variations for a while and then spoke quickly to miss Nakamura, who translated.

"He says your eye is fine," Miss Nakamura told me. "It seems there was an injury about two days ago, but now it is all right."

The doctor prescribed me some eye drops, to be administered six times daily, and then I was free to go. That night, wearing another pair of dark glasses, I headed out into the night. Back at one of the bars, Femme Fatale was there, laughing and pointing at my glasses.

"Why are you wearing sunglasses at night?" came the voice of a random person.

"Yeah this isn't New York you know!" said another unfamiliar voice.

"Black Corey Hart in Japan!" said a third voice.

The faceless men erupted into laughter.

I had no energy to respond to them and Femme Fatale headed back to her group as I sat by the bar, drinking alone for a little while.

* * * *

I've always thought that cities have enough of what a person needs, even if they aren't into crazy things. Once I'm entertained with the right kind of bars and basic entertainment, I'm good to go. I learned this fact for sure when I had the chance to do a writing internship in New York. It was a nice gig, and during four months there, I didn't leave the city once. In fact, that entire time period was spent mostly in a twenty-block radius. I had no desire to see the empire state building, the Statue of Liberty or to go and visit Staten Island. I prowled the Lower East Side like a lone wolf, quite content with its excess of cheap drinks and revolving carousel of amorous locals and foreigners. I sang performance Karaoke on Tuesday nights at a popular dive bar, usually followed by popping into a club next door. On Wednesdays without fail I ate Pad Thai at the same place on 3rd Avenue and enjoyed dollar beers and pizza slices on Thursdays at a bistro near St. Mark's place. On Friday and Saturday I could be found chilling at a punk rock concert in a tiny venue, or musing about life on a rooftop with folks I'd met a few hours earlier on the street. If anything, I wanted my Japanese life to be somewhat similar, but this town was quite different. It took me some time to discover the bars I liked and the routines that fit me. Of course, there were far less offerings day to day in this small town versus a city like New York, but I was still able to do occasional Karaoke with folks near my apartment, where a collection of old truck trailers had been converted into private show rooms. I still ate something every Wednesday, this time instead of Pad Thai I ate tacos and burritos at a restaurant run by a giant Aussie named Chris. On weekends I would make a predictable cycle between a few bars that always had a mix of foreigners and just enough Japanese to keep things entertaining. It was a good time of life, the twenty-something era.

Today was Friday, my favorite day of the week and I am off to a bar called Liquid Kitchen. After an assault of handshakes and hellos I reached the bar counter, nodding at

Carl, the owner. A whiff of strong perfume hit my nose and I saw Femme Fatale beside me.

"Sit beside me," she said, pointing to her table. "Let's talk."

She joked constantly about the scarf I'm wearing. Presently, we were in the last bits of spring and the air was still nippy. My general outfit of choice during this time was a threadbare jacket and a vibrant scarf I received as a gift. The scarf was a loud pink and sewn artfully in a checkered pattern. I wore it on my waist, turned frontward so the knot lay in front of my crotch. It certainly had gotten her attention. She touched it, tugged it and kept laughing at how it brought attention to my lower extremities. I tried to stop her as curious eyes watched her hands moving around my nether regions, but she was very persistent.

"This isn't New York, you know," she said, her green eyes sly and unreadable.

I never understood why she said that, because in our dozens of encounters subsequent to this night, we have never discussed New York, or my brief time there. In fact, I hear 'This isn't New York' said to me in a plethora of random and unrelated situations. In terms of tonight, I don't get her reference because whatever fashion sense I have is *not* based on New York, or having lived there for such a short time. My sense of fashion doesn't go beyond the occasional loud scarf and tight jeans. Maybe I'll be adventurous and wear one of those t-shirts with FCUK on it or something, but that's it. I thought to myself that perhaps New York was just one of those cities, where anything goes and extreme awkwardness, unbridled confidence or things like scarves on your waist which might seem out of the norm elsewhere would be quite fine.

"This isn't Tokyo you know," I mumbled to myself.

Saying that out loud did not feel the same. New York had grit you could taste when the words left your mouth. 'Tokyo' felt clean and sterilized. I could imagine the Ninja turtles roaming in grimy sewers fighting ninjas and mob bosses in the city that never sleeps, but not in Tokyo. The big apple, with its noisy trains and rats dragging pizza into its innards definitely was a place where *things* happened, with the buskers playing songs for money, arrogant wall street guys bumped up on amphetamines sprinting to work and sad vendors trapped in underground stations selling newspapers and cheap candy day in and day out. The appearance of new faces at the table broke this train of thought. They were all friends of Femme Fatale, and all foreigners. The conversation revolved briefly around my scarf and its proximity to my groin then settled on the second-most popular topic for anyone not from Japan originally. *Why do you live and work here?* Tony, the owner of a small club here, gave me a discerning look.

"You live in this city? This is the first time I'm seeing you," he said in a thick Nigerian accent.

He had the steely eyes of a businessman and the smile of a top-billed Vegas stage performer. I could tell he was doing well in life. The other gentleman, also of African descent is named John. "It's just a Christian name," he told me quickly, as if expecting I would assume his name was hard to pronounce or something. After a few drinks the Africans, happy to see a fellow comrade in me, were getting excited. John was talking about Ghana and me.

"I do not care," he said. "You can go into the airport and they will not even need to look at your visa, they will say you are Ghanaian. I have been there, and that is how you look."

"I claimed Ghana a long time ago," I said to the group. "Since all the Jamaican slaves came from there."

For some reason this made everyone at the table erupt in raucous laughter, which confirmed to me that I, and everyone at the table were drunk. The drinks we'd had thus far put me in the mood of an entertainer.

I pointed to John. "He tells me that I look Ghanaian and," I point to Tony. "*He* has the name of my father!"

I left the table laughing in convulsions and went back to the bar, where Femme Fatale sat quietly in an unusually somber state having left us sometime before. I felt the usual mental lull that came with the rapid consumption of alcohol, and I knew the only place I'd be going to soon was my apartment. Everyone in the bar was someone I already knew, and anyone worth meeting had left already.

"I think I'm heading out," I said in a slur. "Everyone here is either married, in a serious relationship, or gay."

Femme fatale took the last point personally and got upset. A nearby friend of hers nearby, whom I'd never met, apparently was gay.

"You are talking too loud man," she said. "In Japan you have to be discreet."

I didn't get it. This was the same Femme Fatale who was on the dance floor at a club last week, being dry humped on the floor by an openly gay man as his friends, a raving group of flaming Brazilians took pictures of the action with their cellphones. It should have dawned on me that her sensitivity was due to the previous round of heavy drinking, but unlike her somber state, I became unusually apologetic, so much so that she got up and went to another side of the bar to avoid my words.

"You are standing too close to me," she said when I went over to talk.

My mind quickly referenced a moment just an hour earlier, when she gave me an unusual disclaimer while playing with the scarf around my waist.

"Your penis means nothing to me," she had said. "I could whip it out, take pictures of it and roll it around. It has no effect."

I couldn't do anything but laugh when she had said this, but her expression was dead serious, all the while her fingers fiddled with the scarf on my waist. As I stood there in her space, trying making my case in the way that beer and tequila enhances one's logic, her best friend appeared, a stocky, square jawed-man well over six feet tall. Fortunately for me, we knew each other well.

"Aw, he just wants to apologize," the big guy said to Femme Fatale.

She said something in reply to him but I heard none of their conversation. Tonight's mission, whatever it was, is over. I mentally calculated the distance from the bar to my house via bike, wondering if I should leave it outside Liquid Kitchen till morning, or attempt a wobbly ride home. I headed out of the establishment, trotting down a narrow flight of stairs out onto the main street. I decided to brave the empty streets on my bike, and sat on it, staring for a moment at the endless, clean pavement that lay before me, through a network of near identical streets back to my apartment. A noise behind me alerted me to someone's presence. It was Femme Fatale.

"I'm not angry with you," she said. "You just have to be more aware of who is around you."

I grumbled an unintelligible response and rode off on my bike. The situation with Femme Fatale annoyed me more than I wanted it to, but I wasn't sure why, and as I turned a corner a block or two from Liquid Kitchen, I slowed the bike to a full stop. A man in a red shirt and khaki pants was running hurriedly away from a building I'd heard was a local brothel. A Japanese woman so fat her clothes could barely contain her bulbous mass was ardently chasing him. Her legs, little tree trunks, took swift, sure steps in pursuit. Giant breasts bounced and quaked with her motions, juggling so violently they threatened to crack her in the jaw. She screamed at him as he scampered away. The man ran in an ailed fashion, from a leg injury or liquor consumption, I wasn't sure. In this dead of night, I was the only witness to this odd theater. Amazingly, the big lady was gaining on the man, and I watched the chase until they disappeared around a corner. Then, I got back on my bike and headed home.

* * * *

Another workweek ended and I was in a pleasant mood. A few of my fellow teachers and I had been on the hip strip earlier, smiling and laughing after an early evening mixer. I'd even met a girl that night, Miko. She had the type of slim frame that I liked, with an endearing face and a long mane of tousled brown hair that fell just past her shoulders. My passable Japanese had worked with her passable English and we genuinely liked each other somewhere in between the broken sentences and awkward laughs. I had broken off from the group to follow Miko back to her train station before meeting back up with them at No Name Bar. She lived a little bit outside the city, and since trains stopped running here around eleven, we decided to meet up another time. She was happy for the company, even though the station wasn't far away. As we walked down the hip strip, my eyes landed on the red lights of a popular red-painted bar above a small restaurant. In this exact moment, I saw Femme Fatale storm out of the bar, discharged with purpose. She went down the steep stairway incredibly fast, two steps at a time, even though she was wearing high heels. A red, stylish dress adorned her figure and I could see that her makeup was a little runny, but I couldn't tell if it was from sweat or tears. A man soon followed out of the entrance, shorter than her, but built like a bricklayer with broad shoulders that showed impressive muscles even through his sport coat. He blustered at her in breathy Japanese, and she responded in like kind, going word for word. The man was incensed but cautious as I noticed him look around a few times as she shouted at him. He straightened up his jacket before re-entering the bar, sprinting up its steep steps like a deer. Femme Fatale stood there for a moment, muttering something, probably curses in her native Russian and then turned around, opposite to myself Miko, not seeing us, and walked up the street, her blonde hair a wisp of moving fire under the streetlights. I felt somewhat driven to follow her, but didn't.

After waving goodbye to Miko at the station, I walked back to the main street, noting that it was just past eleven and still quite early. I stopped at the 7-11 to get a warm up drink to prepare for the madness that would no doubt ensue at the No Name bar where the guys were. When I came outside, a fellow I knew named Yuhei was standing beside the trash receptacle. He was tall, with unusually good looks and had the type of smile that made you immediately feel at ease. Where we had met originally is lost upon me, but we usually ran into each other on this main street, and chatted for a few minutes, mostly about girls. As I drank my beer, he explained to me his method of picking up Japanese women.

"Most times after I meet them I just say 'we will fuck', and that's it," Yuhei said to me.

I laughed in disbelief, but no smile was on his face following that statement. Telepathically confirming this theory, two friends of his, lurking behind us with watchful eyes quickly crossed the street to chat to some girls, with whom after a quick verbal exchange continued walking with them down the road.

"*Nanpa* time," Yuhei said to me with a laugh.

These guys were experts at the instant date, saying hi to the girls walking by, having a drink or two with them at a nearby bar before taking it to a love hotel minutes later. Instinctively, I rubbed my phone in my pocket, wondering if Miko would respond to any messages I sent her tomorrow. I certainly couldn't have an instant date like these late night lotharios. Yuhei and I happened to be standing adjacent to the bar I'd seen Femme Fatale exit from earlier. From that direction I heard a loud shout, which drew my attention to the red staircase. A man's body came flying down the stairs. He hit the ground buttocks first with his feet pointing upwards. His back snapped back and his head smacked the ground. The sound of his head smashing against the pavement sounded like someone took a baseball bat and hit it with all their strength on a concrete wall. To this day I have never heard a sound like it. All activity in the vicinity grinded to a halt. The man lay there, unmoving. Men appeared from the restaurant above, calling to him and running down the stairs. I stepped closer to observe the man, who was about fifty years old in good health, with a muscular chest and a neat buzz cut of salt and pepper hair. Seeing his powerful shoulders and sport coat made me realize that it was the man from earlier, who had been arguing with Femme Fatale. His friends were blubbering in frantic voices. One of the men ran behind him and motioned for the other person to lift him.

"Don't move him!" I shouted at them as they started lifting him. "Yuhei, tell them not to move him because his neck might broken!" I exclaimed.

They looked at me, puzzled and half-mad with fright. Yuhei quickly translated the message and the men let him remain on the ground. His eyelids were fluttering and he seemed semi-coherent. An ambulance eventually came and collected the man, the paramedics moving silently like blue ghosts around him. Once he was on a trolley and pushed into the body of the vehicle, I watched it drive into the distance, swallowed quickly by the thick Saturday night throng. The sound of the ambulance faded, and the din of the street returned. In another minute, there was no indication a man had ever been laying on the floor just feet from where hundreds of people were passing by. Yuhei was not here to witness this part of the night, as he had left to meet his girlfriend, or one of them, at the train station. The incident put me in a somber mood, and I had little interest in going to any more bars after that. As I walked home I kept hearing the thunderous sound of the man's head hitting the pavement over and over, cracking like a bowling ball dropped on cement from high above.

****

Pepsi boy had ended his time of a year in the city, and was having a going away party at a place called Red Rock House. It was filled with people there for the occasion, swathed in dull amber lights, their conversations bubbling out onto the street in a writhing orgy. In attendance of course was Femme Fatale, who at some point came up to me, beaming a bright smile.

"He wants to see it," she said to me.

I groaned.

"What, is this about my scarf again? No," I replied.

"No, he wants to see *it,*" she said with a strange smile.

Femme Fatale looked over her shoulder, and I saw a man approach us. He was tall, muscular and ample, dressed in a black and white suit, his necktie tied around his forehead like a bandana. He pointed a meaty finger at me.

"Show me your magnum," he said.

"What?" I ask.

"Show me your magnum cock size."

His small eyes are a furrowed, unusual expression of intensity. He loomed there for some moments, looking like a lost big brother, or a retired wrestler. I sighed, ignoring the man. My mood was a bit circumspect tonight. I felt as if I was crawling slowly uphill in the hot sun with a life preserver on. In addition to this murk I found myself in, Femme Fatale was in a weird place herself, dropping 'fuck you' to me every other sentence and saying strange things in between each trip she took to the bar. I wondered if her behavior had something to do with the man from the night before, but I didn't ask her. I left where I was sitting.

I went up stairs and chatted with two girls, who I've labeled M number one and M number two because both of their names start with that letter. They were chatting to Texas, the giant man from Turkey, and one a teacher named Dakota, who was from Texas. M number two speaks with an English accent and has a small, round face. Her face is so round in fact; the first thing I imagine upon meeting her is an old porcelain nutcracker toy. To M number one I explained my theory about women who are twenty-five years old.

"Women who are twenty-five that I've met are a little crazy," I said. "Either they want to sleep with everyone under the sun, or get married in a hurry. There doesn't seem to be an in between."

M number two confirmed adamantly that she agreed with me, having already been with quite a few guys under the sun at her ripe old age of twenty-two. I briefly saw an image in my mind of her with a collection of different men, who all marveled at the raw symmetry of her super round face, comparing it to the moon, marbles and the eyes of owls.

"I think that is a good theory," M number one replied. "The question is, which type of twenty-five am I?"

I did not get the chance to answer her question because I was called to the upstairs Karaoke booth. Loud squeals greeted me when I entered the room. The Aussie girls that were in Tokyo every other week were all in attendance tonight, sitting in a trio in the booth.

"We never see you!" one of them chimed in a heavy accent.

I smiled and nodded. One of them, a tall girl with generous hips and freckles gave me a sly eye. Since the day we arrived a year ago, she had consistently worn the same hairstyle of closely trimmed razor sharp bangs. "I can dance like the black girls," she had said to me many moons ago, upon our first meeting.

Presently, these girls feel familiar only in appearance. I know nothing about them beyond a few night adventures and loud conversations over beers. As I looked around at all the people here to wish Pepsi Boy adieu it dawned on me they all kept in touch pretty well. I'd heard some of the many wild stories about partying in Kyoto and Tokyo, orgies in *Ryokans* and tales of people running out on massive Sushi bills. They were living the kind of Japanese lifestyle that seemed fun and natural for a foreigner. Stuff you laughed about over a cup of coffee or a few beers. Stuff you told your kids one day.

I did an okay rendition of a Linkin Park song. The crowd applauded me when I finished and I bowed slightly then left the room. People were saying they wanted to take the party to a nearby club, called Pluto. I knew the club, and it wasn't a far walk from Pepsi boy's party, so I decided to go.

A crowd of smaller than usual Japanese folk packed the dance floor and tonight I felt no thrill around them, towering like a lanky beast in their midst. In the corner of the dance floor, I saw Femme Fatale. She was with some of the guys from Pepsi Boy's party. They swarmed around her like flies as she danced, her hair billowing like a blonde flag. Her outfit was a perfect fit for her body, tight and black accentuating all the excess and hiding any shortcomings. In the awkwardness of our many encounters I realized I'd never really *looked* at her.

She had a long and graceful neck, a captivating bosom, delicate musician's hands and a somewhat curvy but not overly voluptuous figure. In this moment as she danced, hypnotizing the men around her on purpose I truly saw her for the first time. The girl who was mean and surly and confusing and cursed a lot was now a clear image. Like I, it seemed that her captive audience had all come to this realization in their own way, trapped in their rapt adoration of her while she performed for them. The men present were all tethered to her, including me; by a previous snarky comment, a memory of doing shots at some bar, somewhere, or at one of the dozens of scenarios where she came into the room in a loud outfit on a mission to do something dirty that night. One of the guys, sleepy eyed Jim, she grabbed roughly by his beard and pulled him towards her. From my angle on the dance floor, she had direct eye contact with me. He could hardly believe his luck, as he immediately started awkwardly gyrating his hips off beat to the music. Femme Fatale gripped his hips tightly, calming his ill-timed bucking. She clasped him in a sway, the entire time looking at me. I could not read her eyes, because the lights in the club made them shiny and black, as if they had emerged from some alien lagoon. But there was also desire in them, flooding out like the lights around us, spreading like a growing bubble. I could feel it on the tips of my fingers, crawling up like ants, making the hairs on my arm stand up. I could see the fine blonde hairs on her neck even from this distance in the dim light, her toned thighs pressing hard against Jim's old Dockers. She locked her eyes with mine as she danced with him for an eternity. Then she started kissing Jim. Sloppy and loud, all tongue and heavy breath, all the while starting at me. The tingling in my fingertips left me in a puff of hot breath. A heat of another kind stirred in my stomach and I left the club, angry and alone. It was in this cloud of rage I ran into Miko.

"Hey!" she said to me. "Did you get my messages?"

"Messages?" I asked.

I fished my phone from my pocket and checked my e-mails. Sure enough, there was one from her saying something about going to Pluto. I must have missed hearing the notification sound while singing Karaoke at the previous party.

"Do you mind going somewhere else?" I asked.

She said that was fine, and we walked through a few sparsely occupied back streets, to a tiny bar I'd never been to. Inside there was a counter with enough space for about four people, a dart board by the entrance next to a digital jukebox and an old TV connected to a Super Nintendo. Plugged into the ancient game console was a faded *Street Fighter* cartridge. She immediately challenged me to a match. I considered myself a reasonably good player having put in at least a decade of practice with such games in my youth, but she proceeded to give me the kind of brutal beating that could make a grown man cry. We laughed a lot as we played and I found myself now devoid of the anger I'd felt so strongly earlier at the club. Miko, dressed in a conservative gray sweater a size too large looked quite nice. I paid particular attention to her fingers, small and delicate as she clasped her glass of beer and took sips in between rounds, her tiny lips shiny. We had more conversations in broken Japanese and English about Jamaica, Japan and reggae music. She showed me pictures of a trip she took to Malaysia, focusing on a photograph of her standing under a coconut tree with a guy with dreadlocks.

"He looks like you!" she said with a laugh.

The man in the image was chubby, significantly shorter than me with a lighter complexion and a face that bore absolutely no resemblance to mine.

"Very true!" I replied.

Miko told me soon afterward that her train would be coming soon since it was almost eleven. In a repeat of the night before I began the process of walking her to her train stop. As we took the main street towards the terminal, we observed a man engaging in a strange activity. In front of a *Pachinko* gaming salon, he was sprinting rapidly back and forth, fifteen or twenty feet at a time, all the while screaming *aaaaah!* at the top of his lungs. He was truly committed to this task, as each yelp sounded like his lungs would burst from sheer exertion. Miko chuckled and pinched my back, and indication to keep walking forward.

"Japan is crazy," I said to her.

"Of course! This isn't New York you know," Miko replied.

I nodded in agreement, and followed her down the road and through the crowds, to the train station.

The Lady at The Beach

I never believed in ghosts until I came to Japan. When some things happened that made me think ghosts might be real, my reaction wasn't what I expected. You think you might scream, or run in fright, but it is actually quite different from that. I can't explain it really, but I can tell you what happened. I'd come to Japan like most twenty-something year olds, to teach English and escape the west for a while. Mind you, I wasn't one of those Asian fetishists (there were several in my training group) that came to Japan to rage in the bedrooms of as many Japanese women as they could. Mine was a different sort of journey, as I often found myself in roaming pabulum each day after work, shambling in a slow shuffle around the protracted edges of my small town and it's mysterious innards. I spent hours at a moody and ancient castle, absorbing its green tinged walls and exquisite sculptures, most of which had the expression of the bereaved; scowls and contemplative faces, frozen in leaps and ponderous positions. Well-tended trees were my friends, whispering mysteries to the wind and myself, as I took in the pungent scent of pine and old dust. I'd sit on surly benches with a book in hand, often wondering why I embraced solitude in these moments over company. Heck if I knew.

They say Japan teaches you about yourself in different ways. It can be a place of incredible depth and insight, which for some reveals to them the darkest parts of who they are. It isn't merely the language barrier that troubles the twenty-something year old mind, but the realization that they are alone, in language, culture, and often companionship. It is an exquisite, fractured isolation, which for some is too much. During my training with several of the budding teachers and fetishists I heard a story about a young recruit who for some reason, started setting fire to newspapers and throwing them off the second floor balcony of the school he was teaching at. This was during the day at eleven AM, the equivalent of rush hour for English teachers here. From what I heard, he was giggling and screaming the entire time he threw the burning material over the balcony, a victim of seeing his true self trapped in the infinitely gilded cage of a boring Junior high school. Another girl, legendary initially for her insatiable libido and predilection for chasing effete young Japanese men, left after three months because she couldn't handle living in her designated town, which consisted of a few unimpressive farms and one bar populated mostly by old men with wives tales and no wives to tell them to. Where I lived fortunately was in an area called *nana,* the center of the city, which had enough vibrancy to keep a man my age from spiraling completely into to an abyss of complete boredom. I spent lots of time at a local video arcade called *Taito Station,* intermittently downing alcoholic beverages and furtive snacks that one can only get in Japan, playing *Street Fighter* ad nauseam. There, surrounded by machines screaming with color and garbled lights I would be elsewhere, me and the digital sprites on screen my salvation from monotony, as I shot *hadoukens* at my enemies and pretended I was truly a globe-trotting martial arts expert. Gaijin bars, a label for bars that cater to foreigners who may not speak much Japanese, were also a regular option. Decorated in the simple fashion of dark wood and simple accoutrements I spent hours chatting about nothing and everything with some of the bar owners, mostly Australian or Englishmen who came to Japan decades ago and had long settled down. A regular complaint from them was the phenomenon of the "Japanese curse", whereby once a Japanese woman had a child, they apparently lost all interest in sex with their husbands and was more interested in the pressing issues of motherhood. This must have been shocking for them I thought, most likely having the initial encounter of being the fresh new blonde guy in town they were running around with. I would listen to these men tell me these stories with a buzz in my eyes and a simple smile. I can't even imagine a woman loving me, much less wanting to marry me and have children. The ending to these conversations was usually unceremonious, and my next move would be to trot home if I didn't take my bike with me that night. Alas it was Saturday and there was no need for me to worry about stumbling into work trying to pretend I wasn't drunk, so I went to a bar nearby called Pluto. This was the night I saw the ghost for the first time.

The crowd is thin, but the music is good, and no one bats an eye at me as I walk in, even though I'm not Japanese. The place fits me, with its emphasis on shadows and a dimly lit bar, patrons that favor the dark more than the light. Paraphernalia about outer space and science fiction are here and there; a tattered poster of the Milky Way raised high over a sleepy shelf, a vase behind the DJ booth adorned with a painting of Yoda expertly done across its breadth; little flying saucers on the bar. The folks on the dance floor move in a tight rhythm of youthful expression; kids with perfectly coiffed hair swaying left to right, their bodies virtually indistinguishable in the shadows. They are the remnants of the night, detritus washing ashore to be discovered later. I head to the bar, and sit. The bartender here is a friendly guy named Daisuke, who speaks passable English. He has an average but pleasant face, with a bleached shock of blonde hair hanging permanently over one eye, the rest pulled into a tight bun. I'm already a little tipsy from the Gaijin bar before, so I ask him for a Daiquiri. *Da-ka-ree?* He replies with a slight frown.

"A Daiquiri," I say to him, "Is a sweet drink. It usually has strawberries in it, or some kind of fruit. You blend it with vodka, ice and a little sugar."

Daisuke nods at me, somewhat understanding. Japanese courtesy dictates that even if one does not fully understand what someone else is saying, one does not immediately respond with supposed confusion. To do so would be impolite. So, Daisuke turns around and starts to blend something based on what he perceives to be my instructions. The music is unusually good tonight despite the thin crowd, and I close my eyes for a moment, feeling the whiskey, beer and vodka course through my system as I float far away. What I do is akin to hopping on a raft from place to place; watching eddies and tides with a drink in my hand, hoping I find my next destination. I know that my constant motions equate to restlessness, and that I should start working on making real friends soon. But, I like this bar and places like it, with its smothering dark space, where everything in front of me is somewhat predictable. A stream of people enter the bar fresh from another event and I recognize some faces from around town. There is Taji, a DJ with waist-length dreadlocks I've seen at a few parties. He's here with his girlfriend; I think her name is Ayumi and another person from his crew who calls himself Gully. The other faces I do not recognize but they are also remnants of the night, happy to appear in this place because there is nothing else to do. Behind me, Daisuke seems to have given up on trying to make me a Daiquiri and I order a gin and tonic instead. He makes it incredibly strong, but I like the burn on my tongue, a quick sip bringing me back to life like a match lighting up a dark empty room. He laughs as I grimace joyfully, and asks me to give him the instructions for making a Daiquiri properly before I leave. I nod ambivalently and drift to the dance floor, summoned to it. My shoulders move of their own accord in this space with the energetic Japanese beside me, all of us in our own hidden shadow world. The name Pluto fits here, because we could have been anywhere; watching an exquisite solar event on a moon base while raving in zero gravity, or on Pluto itself, in some kind of Kubrickian space station, getting wasted while watching meteor showers through a twenty-inch thick window, safe from space's naked vacuum. Music plays louder and the gin and tonic fuels me with energy. I rarely dance, but I'm rocking with a bit more gusto tonight. I take another sip of my drink, detecting a flurry of activity beside me. Two gorgeous girls with slim bodies and incredibly long brown hair rush past me with the energy of the night, talking loudly, coasting on a sea of giggles and makeup. One catches my eye, and I feel a twinge of excitement. The night before, on Friday I think I met one of them on my solo partying circuit around town. She beams a giant smile at me. I smile and walk over.

"Hug," I say to her.

"*Nani?*" she replies.

I said it again, a bit slower and broken into Japanese phonetics.

"*Ha-goo,*" I say.

Her eyes process what I said for a split second and then she hugs me with strong little arms, and I realize I've actually never met her before. No matter. An equal realization was that for her to hug me, a foreigner, not knowing who I am might, *might* indicate that she was quite intoxicated.

"Hi," she says exasperatedly.

"Hey," I reply.

She is quite pretty, with a subdued sort of movie actress look. The type of beauty that certain leading ladies have without being overly voluptuous or buxom. She wore what looked like a shiny green onesie, but I'm not good with fashion, so I wasn't sure. Her friend smiled as I talked to her, but said nothing to us and turned to Daisuke, engaging him in conversation.

"Where you from?" she says to me.

"Jamaica." I reply.

"Really?"

She said this with absolute surprise, in the way a child who swore he failed a test realizes he actually has received an A and does not know why. I told her I was a designer. Incidentally, I am wearing one of my own shirts. Technically I am just dabbling in design, and had the shirt I was wearing printed at a local print shop, but the gin and tonic gives me a bit more posh and pomp at this time of night.

"I want to buy one," she says, rubbing my chest. "I am a mother!" she exclaims triumphantly.

"Very cool," I reply. "One child?"

"Yes, I have one. But I am twenty-one!"

She says this with a bright expression. I held her hand beckoning her to twirl. "Very nice." I said to her, admiring her slim body. A sudden wave of fright shot through my veins, as I worried about my uncharacteristic metamorphosis into a late night lothario.

"You think I am nice?" she asks me, eyes filled with liquor and much more.

"Yes, you are," I reply.

"Let's get another drink," she says, turning to Daisuke and chirping at him in bullet Japanese.

He laughs and winks at me before turning to get our drinks, whatever they are. Maybe tonight is my night, I think to myself. One of those nights where the shadows are welcoming with the promise of a naked body beside mine and a new story for me to tell myself, because I have no real friends to share it with. Sometimes I hang out with the guys from my training group, but they are scattered all over the prefecture and besides a handful of girls from Australia who seem to travel every weekend to Tokyo, I haven't met that many other foreigners to spend time with. This girl, whatever her name is, reminds me of my last such encounter a few weeks ago with a girl named Mika.

"Here you go!" she says, pushing a drink into my hand with gusto.

It is another incredibly strong gin and tonic, and we say *kampai,* clink glasses face to face and head to the dance floor. Her friend seems to have disappeared, but it doesn't matter. It is just us on the dance floor, swaying like the breeze, our drinks in hand. This last drink has made me quite confident and I suggest heading back to my place and she agrees with little contemplation. There is no mention of her being a mother or having a child and we leave hand in hand, stepping into the night. The darkness of Pluto evaporates as we step outside onto the well-lit main street. Cars and people with night energy meander about, looking for the next thrill. She reaches into her bag and pulls out a small camera, pointing it at me. The LCD flashes brightly as snaps with a loud whirr. She shows me the picture, completely blurry with only a street light in focus behind us. I laugh and tell her its perfect. This is when she tells me her name is Ayano.

The street I live on is a bit dark and extremely quiet because it is a typical Japanese neighborhood. Ayano tells me she loves dark streets, which should immediately raise red flags in my mind but only makes me chuckle. I'm cruising in the moment, lost in the little details I'm trying to figure out about her; the softness of her skin against mine, how she looks naked, and if I'll see her again after this. These images run through my mind at a gallop and I sneak a brief peck on her lips, sending a shot of warmth through my body. It is then I see a woman standing the center of the road. She has a giant ribbon in her hair, which is much larger than her head and she is wearing a bright red polka dot dress. Shards of dark hair cover her eyes, and the glow of the streetlights gives her skin an orange tint. When she looks up, my blood runs cold. Her eyes, if one would call them that, have nothing in them. They are devoid of emotion and life and project a frigid, naked energy. I freeze. Ayano, following my momentum, stops awkwardly. She pinches my stomach and asks me why I stopped so quickly. I look at her cute movie star face and then back at the road, but the woman is gone.

"Come, come!" Ayano says a loudly, which makes me look around nervously at neighboring apartments.

Still thinking about the woman I saw before, I survey the area a few times and see nothing but the murky gloom of quiet streets, illuminated by light beams shining from upright streetlamps that resemble watchful soldiers.

"You didn't see that lady?" I ask her.

"What lady?" Ayano says with a chirp. "The only lady right here is *meee!*"

My apartment is nearby, and we enter the studio and immediately get to the meat of the matter; she on me smelling like sweets and candy, me hard and gin-fueled, our motions orchestrated by the backdrop of some random musical playlist on my laptop. After a few sweaty encounters, most of the alcohol has escaped through our pores and it turns out we actually like one another. Her English is vastly better than I remember it sounding at Pluto, and after our romp we watch *Back To The Future* on my laptop and fall asleep in each other's arms.

I dream, and it in I'm back at Pluto, but no one is there. A halting feeling comes to mind, the kind where you are not sure if you are dreaming or awake. It is often a missing or extra detail that reveals this to us; impossible weather conditions like a neon sky, or things in places they aren't supposed to be, like an upstairs bedroom where the kitchen is supposed to be. It is obvious to me that I am at club Pluto, but it is different. The space is double its usual size and devoid of the Sci-Fi paraphernalia. The air is a thick blanket of musty air. Music is playing from somewhere but I cannot see a DJ deck, darkness greets me from every angle. I shout out hello and hear nothing in response. The dark swallows my voice with each attempt, swelling and growing with each utterance from my mouth. Shadows around me begin twitching erratically, the music now unusually loud. Then the lights come on with a *poof* and in front of me is the lady with the giant ribbon, pink now, her hair over her eyes. She takes a few stilted steps towards me but I cannot move. Closer and closer she comes, all the while her face is held low, chin on her neck. Then she starts to slowly look up at me and I am overwhelmed by fright. Bright light greets me as I open my eyes. It's morning and I instinctively look beside me, seeing that Ayano isn't there. I feel a brief panic grip my chest, the same sensation I felt with the last girl I'd been with. In a similar scenario I'd woken up in the morning and she was gone, save the lingering scent on the bed of our passionate night before, and hints of her perfume on my t-shirt, which lay in a crumpled heap on the floor. I didn't get her number that night and hadn't seen Mika since. A noise from the bathroom accompanied by a flushing noise clears my doubts.

Ayano appears in moments afterwards, strolling confidently towards me in a matching pair of Dolce & Gabbana bra and panties.

"Daijyoubu?" she asks me. "Sounds like you had a nightmare maybe."

"Yes," I'm fine, I reply.

We sit on the bed and she pulls her camera out of her bag. She shows me pictures of her and a friend on a recent trip to Jamaica. I'm quite surprised by this, but then have a brief memory of her maybe mentioning that fact at Pluto, when I was more focused on dancing and trying to sneak a kiss. I laugh to myself, figuring this is the reason why she had such a significant interest in me. We hug as she scrolls through pictures on the LCD screen of her Fuji camera. Spots I know from Kingston pop up. There is a photo of her and the same friend from Pluto standing by giant speakers at a place I knew was the Stone Love head quarters for a party called Weddy Wednesdays. In the next one she stands in a sumo style pose grinning madly in a bikini on a beach called Lime Quay. The last picture is quite sexual, showing her and her friend simultaneously licking a large chocolate ice cream cone at what I assumed to be a place in Kingston called Devon House. Throughout this slideshow I feel a light calm energy from her. She smiles, puts down the camera and we kiss, falling into each other once more.

We eat breakfast at a nearby Denny's and plan to meet up the next day. My friend is having a barbeque at his house somewhere outside the city and she wants to accompany me. As I walk her to the train station and marvel at the beauty of the day; gorgeous white clouds skating across the vast blue sky I feel nervous. My days on surly benches with trees for company might be gone, held in the promise of this little body beside me. I listen to her tell me about her creative aspirations and why she loves traveling. I nod and smile, ignoring the pounding in my chest. Maybe this is my fate, I think. A drunken dalliance with a cute girl named Ayano might foreshadow my permanent stay in Japan. Maybe I'll open my own Gaijin bar and tell war stories to a fresh-faced twenty-something year old a decade from now, who knows.

It does not take long for the high of the night to wane, and the dark materials from my past to begin singing to me in a cacophony of doubt. There is no reason for her to like me, I muse, noticing an irritability rise within me in the way that only a person annoyed with himself experiences. I make a pit stop at a convenience store a few minutes from my apartment. Like all of them I've seen, it has extremely welcoming bright lettering, a clean interior and the promise of good food, an assortment of fantastic snacks and of course, alcoholic beverages. A gust of cool air hits my face as I walk in. *Irrashaimasae!* came the voice of a worker attending to something on a shelf. I buy a long icy can of beer and go back to my apartment. A cloud follows me while I think of the strange woman with the ribbon, an eerie feeling swirling in the chamber of my stomach. There is no doubt that I saw her. This is what I meant in the beginning that seeing a ghost can give one a sensation you don't immediately react to. Why the ribbons? And why was she there? When I return to my apartment, it does not feel the same. It is cavernous and void. Ayano was my second visitor in months and I did not realize how pleasant it was to have company. My days mindlessly reading English to Japanese children and meandering around town high on sticky snacks and whiskey was no longer joyous by contrast. The room feels like those eyes I'd seen the night before, lifeless, vacant. I begin taking off my shoes when an icy chill bursts in the air, hitting me like water thrown from a bucket. My air conditioning is off, and I haven't opened my cold beer yet. Goosebumps leap from my arms and I quickly leave the apartment, heading for the safety of my other lair, the video arcade.

I am used to the city now, and it is not as imposing as it once was. When I first arrived, observing its layout felt like looking at an exquisite work of art, with its bone-clean cobbled streets, colorful stores and cornucopia of cake and stationery shops. That day when I stood with my two suitcases in hand with the city before me; the effect was sharp, like the crusted skin of a wild beast brushing your hand, or that sensation one gets right after leaping into icy water. Everything was obvious and clear; the height of the buildings, the lack of readable road signs and the Japanese *Kanji* characters imported from China, loud, black and ubiquitous, screaming at my ignorance in being unable to read them, flanked by giant exclamation marks flanked or adorably designed *chibi* characters. I came to Japan because Kingston had lost its sensation for me. To my family, I had attempted to explain that my days felt repetitive and I was stuck in a weird kind of kaleidoscopic time warp. I woke up everyday and looked towards the mountains and knew where they ended. My friends all had similar jobs, some with families already and I could see their lives fast forward thirty or forty years, with them on their deathbeds, surrounded by their weeping, now grown children in a room filled with certificates and decorations from their predictable, previous life. Often in Kingston, in the middle of the city walking down a hot road I could smell the sea, but it was a sea I knew; green and blue tinted, lukewarm after one pm and cold by five. The music that played on the beach, whichever beach, was always the same and the families scattered about, bodies blackened by the sun never inspired me to want the same. The little children screaming at their mothers for ice cream or wreaking havoc with sand wars did not thrill me, nor did I ever go to the beach often. There, I did not have my kindly Japanese castle with its surly benches for company, but I had streets with lights and people milling about, weekly parties where men dance fervently all night chasing the same women, waking up to the same reality. I could not see this reality becoming anything different in my mind, save the stamps of time, a little more wear and tear under my eyes, weakness in joints that previously were invulnerable. Women had little interest in me, and when a friend, John took his own life, the city became a haunted town. He followed me everywhere we had been together before, standing with a flat smile in the shadows, his hand on my back but not there. When I went on the plane I felt nothing when Jamaica was disappearing behind me, and I felt nothing much when I landed twenty-two hours later. I hadn't felt much during this journey In Japan as well, not until tonight. Until Ayano.

****

Bill is a tall man of considerable girth made for a life in the woods. He sometimes looks comically out of place when I see him in the city, strolling barrel-chested throughout this world of generally slimmer folk. It makes sense that he would be inclined to live outside the city, near the sea and trees, a place made for men like him. He runs an organization that is responsible for cleaning a long stretch of the beach near his home. It is a simple activity to get involved with. One wears gloves and gets bags and takes up garbage from the beach, then afterwards meets up with the group for a large barbeque and drink up. It was this event that I had invited Ayano to. I've been to at least three of these events before, enjoying myself but generally staying in the background, noticing the guys from my group with their fresh new Japanese girlfriends, giddy with the promise of what may come. I busied myself at these events drinking beer, talking about books with Bill and generally avoiding the other couples. Sometimes, I'd cross the road and head into the enclave of trees blanketing the perimeter of the beach, but I was always afraid to go too far in the dark by myself. I'd look back and see the dim light of Bill's house and prefer the warmth and promise of beer than the naked isolation of strolling on an empty beach.

Though in his early thirties, Bill had the wizened sensibility of one much older. One night after one of these events, we sat in his library with his girlfriend and her colleague, a girl from Israel who lived in Yokohama. Much of the house he'd built from scratch, with carefully selected and hand-smoothed ply boards, petrified wood and other components, and I marveled at his craftsmanship. This was a man who lived solidly in his own idea of reality, in the way his body and size projected an aura of stability and power, so too was his house. Books had always been my friends, and there we were, surrounded by them, as rain and wind mauled the windows, preventing me from going to the bus stop.

"I know what you are feeling," he said to me that evening.

"What am I feeling?" I replied, taking a sip of my umpteenth beer.

"It's that feeling of drifting on a raft with nowhere to stay," Bill said with a smile.

I didn't respond, listening to thunder rumbling outside, as if agreeing with Bill.

"You'll be fine though, Japan has a way of revealing to us who we really are," Bill said.

"Cheers to that," I had said, raising my beer.

I didn't feel much better after he said that, but felt more comfort in what I saw out the window, flashes of lightning near a raging sea, with the trees bowing at the mercy of the wind. I saw myself out there, running and screaming, battling with the sky.

The video arcade has less people there than I expect as I walk in. A sleepy-looking guy is playing street fighter on the stack of machines meant to accommodate six people at a time. His eyes smile more than his lips as he sees me walk in. I'm immediately calmer, the warble of the arcade machines like friendship to my ears. I take my space at one of opposite *Street Fighter* machines, relishing the satisfying clink of my fifty-yen coin as it drops in its slot, signaling the our warfare. Despite the noise of the arcade, I am in solitude. I sit here as I do at school when I'm not teaching classes. In the main school building, away from the gymnasium there is a place upstairs just before a staircase that takes you to the roof, called the *Eigo Room*. We teach special classes there, with the lights turned off and everyone dead silent for thirty minutes. Despite the room being literally named, the "English Room", I tend to be in there sitting through documentaries (all in Japanese) about old Samurai, esoteric Japanese history, or a revolution no one really cares about anymore. When I am free, on days devoid of activity and noise, I go there. The windows are covered and taped with brown paper to create the darkness that immerses one when watching a film. This gives me some modicum of privacy, because no teacher has a private space here, and must share their space publicly at all times with other teachers.

I smash a few buttons and watch as my character gets defeated in a hail of projectiles from my opponent. I smile; take a sip on the alcoholic beverage I snuck into the arcade in a brown bag and drop in another fifty-yen coin. At school, things are monotonous and predictable. There are the same classes every Thursday and Friday, morning assemblies and happy hour on Wednesday. The routine stands in front of you like the girl you already slept with, all her parts exposed and no longer a thrill to experience. All of your feelings are now aligned to something else, but one day you get bored, idle or frustrated. You realize that your simple schedule is sapping a portion of your life experience. The work you do to ensure that you have a place to live and eat is also, possibly not where you want to be. Some days might be fun, but they all won't be. There will be days you want to toss your files into the air, throw your tie in the toilet and hit flush. Then you'll want to run outside, smiling gleefully and run naked through a public park. You won't do this, but you'll think about what you want to be. You're still young, you say. There's still time. Maybe you'll be a rock star or a famous writer. Maybe you'll spearhead a new tech company and be a billionaire in a manner of years. You could be a travel writer that does dangerous assignments, and joke in broken Portuguese with guys you barely know about that girl you slept with in high school. Or you could take that really interesting route—TV personality. You could be the next Howie Mandel or Chris Rock; getting a thousand hits on a grainy YouTube video where you chat about that time you got booed at a comedy club in Philly. Or maybe you'll be a game programmer, like those MIT kids who came up with Guitar Hero. Maybe you could just be a bum after winning the lottery, sitting home idly buying whatever you feel like, and only date women in Paris, even though you live in New York. Maybe you could do all these things, but then you wake up.

You are at work, and you've been fantasizing. The voices around you coalesce into an onerous din. Closing your eyes doesn't help, and thinking about escaping won't help you either. Someone walks beside you and taps you on the shoulder. "Hey, we have a meeting in ten minutes," they say. You smile and nod, but inside you want to be in Bali, walking with a cute chick on the beach. You want to be in Senegal, snapping pictures of dancers with crystal dark skin. You want to be in Germany, running your hand across the Berlin wall, snapping pictures with tall blonde people and asking questions from a five-dollar phrase book. Alas, you can't. You are at work, and you have a contract. The most you can look forward to are holidays and weekends, and you eye the calendar with anticipation as each day crawls along. You can plan ahead, and squeeze some trips into that three-day week, or those five days of sick leave you never take. You sit happily and fantasize about that two-day trip to Disney World you'll take, but know you'll probably just sleep in. You sigh as inevitability hits you. This office is as much your home as your actual one.

Maybe that's what happened to the English teacher who went crazy and burned those newspapers, I think to myself, celebrating my victory on the arcade machine this time around. Maybe he wanted to be all those things and it drove him mad. All he could see was the predictable path before him, the days revolving like a hamster wheel, slowly consuming him like fire to paper. I certainly have not reached this point yet, but sometimes I fear reaching there. A relationship can make that easier. You go through your day of repetitive activity, but out there, somewhere is someone thinking about you. She wants to feel your touch at night, and smell your body next to hers. She wants to have those fleeting moments with you, even if work is at 8 AM the next day. For her, you will be a priority, and that might make things more palatable. You'll sit in a meeting and smirk inwardly about the comment she made the night before when you went out to dinner. You will blush when raw sexual memories spring up at not-so opportune moments. You will let out a heavy breath when something happens and you get pissed off with some idiot on the road, or a belligerent fellow who doesn't like foreigners, but you know that your baby will be there to make you feel better later. You will wake up at the crack of dawn, ready to work, knowing that under the stillness of the morning sky, when we come to life, she's out there, and maybe after she brushes her teeth, a thought of you will pop into her head, and she'll smile. This keeps you going, that is, if she even exists.

Day turns into night after I have long left the arcade. I'm roaming again in the small confines of the city, working hard to ignore the memory of that strange chill in my studio apartment. I don't normally do much on a Saturday night, and have little interest in conversations at one of the Gaijin bars. I stock up on liquor at the convenience store, ensuring that I will at the very least, eventually, be unaware of anything strange happening at home. I arrive to the familiar doorway, with its arms open and wide. Inside still feels cold and naked, dry like a forgotten towel on a hot roadside. Time passes in a blur as I drink and watch movies on my laptop, feeling unease battle my need to sleep. I nod off a few times, despite the bright lights everywhere. Fear has turned me into a child, and the apartment is lit like Christmas. Even the bathroom light is on. I fall asleep soon enough and darkness envelops me for a while. Then during a fitful sleep I feel something strong grab my leg.

I rise up from my futon, my body a damp mess, signaling a sleep of wet turmoil. I am seized with an unusually granite hardness, despite being cloaked with fear. I see nothing around me, but notice immediately that the lights are off. Cold sweat washes down my neck as I turn the lights back on. I hurriedly put on some clothes and leave the apartment in sweatpants with my key in hand, into the Japanese night. A few shapes float about, people going in and out of their homes, lifeless husks with silhouettes I will never know. I walk slowly down the road, savoring the bright lights beaming from Seiyu, which is a large Japanese supermarket. The light makes me feel better as I walk around for a bit. It is too late or early to go to any video arcades. In actuality I am not sure what time it is. I don't have the habit of wearing a watch and I left my phone in the house. The light beckons to me and I stay in her bosom, occasionally looking back, seeing nothing, but patches of black.

****

Ayano drives a cute automobile that resembles a gray box. She beams at me as she picks me up by my place. I couldn't help but smile seeing her in the driver's seat, her energy bound tight like a bow ready to be released. We drive through the contiguous streets of the city out onto wide highways flanked by sweeping plains and rice fields. Warm sea air blows through the open car windows and Ayano plays dancehall music on her radio while peppering me with questions about what I think about Japan. Every few minutes, that creeping feeling of worry spreads through my chest when I look at the wind blowing her hair, and wonder about the carefree smirk on her lips. My chest feels tight and firm, like whatever grabbed my leg in the dark last night. Despite how I feel, whenever she smiles at me, I smile back.

At Bill's place, we park up the street and meet the group at the house. The usual suspects are there; English teachers I'd trained with and their giddy girlfriends, some of Bill's Japanese friends and a few other long time ex-pats who'd lived and settled down in Japan. Bill breaks down the goals of the organization and what we are expected to do in a quick meeting, and then we head to the beach. We grab a large set of garbage bags and walk for a few minutes through a dense enclave of wild trees to the beach. Just like first time I went to this beach, seeing the sea in my vision fills me with a sense of calm. It is a familiar face. Ayano hits it off with Bill and his girlfriend, while I, still a bit moody and pensive, distract myself by walking and talking with other members of the group, picking up garbage and sorting into different bags. We have red bags and blue bags. "Red is for unburnable, blue for burnable," Bill told the group earlier. We were also all commissioned old straw hats, pairs of well-used gloves and a few plastic bags each. With only two colours of bags, people still ask during the clean which is which. I was putting the non-burnables in the red bag, which luckily for me, was correct.

It is good to be around people, watching them play with Bill's dog, Chai, laugh with each other and work with gusto to clean up the beach. No one would ever call me an environmentalist, but I enjoy the work and ensure to have a few bags full by the time we are ready for the evening barbeque. The blue sky is a dream and I find myself laughing with a few of my colleagues and their girlfriends, Ayano occasionally works alongside me to pick up detritus, telling me about her life in between dropping off loads. It is sweaty, fulfilling work, and I am famished by barbeque time. I wolf down a few plates of *Yaki Tori* and drink some water. Ayano is happily chatting to a few of the guys from my training group, along with Bill's girlfriend. This is at the front of the house, and I exit that area and walk towards Bill's sizeable yard, heading to the garden, near the rear of the house. I'm cleaning my teeth with a napkin when something gives me pause.

Standing in the garden, is a breathtakingly attractive girl. She is wearing a white purple skirt that fits her contours perfectly, and a sleek top that battles to hide the swell of her breasts. Moonlight reflects in slow, moving ripples on her jet-black hair. She is standing casually, looking at some of Bill's flowers, which stand in a straight row of clay coloured pots. As if knowing she was being observed, she turns to me. Striking eyes blazing with a fiery potency meet mine and make me catch my breath. She smiles in this moment, and the fire like quality of her eyes calms down. She gestures for me to come over.

"Do you know this plant?" she asks me.

I look at the plant, and it looks like every plant I've seen before in my life. Green, with leaves, in a pot.

"Sorry, I'm not sure what it is," I say somewhat sheepishly.

"I don't either, but for some reason it held me with its quality," she says.

She speaks with a motherly fondness, and I am forced to believe her sentiments. Apparently, she had just arrived to the house, unable to come to the cleanup earlier due to a previous obligation. Her reasons for being here in the garden alone were never discussed, but she explained to me why she spoke fluent English, having come from a family that had constantly traveled during her childhood. They had lived in Taiwan, Singapore and London during her childhood, so in addition to English and Japanese she spoke Cantonese and Mandarin as well.

"I've always been drawn to gardens," she says to me.

She reaches out and holds my hand. Hers is warm and soft and I am surprised by my reaction; a warm feeling galloping through my chest, mixed with a stir of worry that Ayano might see me.

"I'm sorry, I like to hold hands, it's just a habit of mine," she says smiling broadly.

"It's fine I say," gently releasing her hand.

We sit on a small bench for a few minutes and exchange pleasantries. She's quite funny, telling me anecdotes from her journeys about men who've tried to woo her and getting sick on a bus while traveling through South America. She'd read a lot of books and had one to recommend to me that she lent to Bill sometime before.

"It's called the Confederacy of Dunces, have you read it?"

"No," I reply.

"It's an amazing book," she says, her eyes drifting upwards, to the moon.

"Why do you like the book?" I ask.

"More than just the book I think it is the story of the writer I find fascinating. His name was John Kennedy Toole, and he wrote this book shortly before he killed himself. Not only did the book go on to become a mainstream hit, it also earned Mr. Toole a posthumous Pulitzer Prize. I read the book during a trip to Vietnam, and I realized I was holding an unrealized work in my hands. That is to say, the writer had no idea his work would ever reach so far, sell so many copies and win the most coveted writing prize in America. Toole died not knowing his true worth and relevance in this world.

I think that, more than anything makes the work even more incredible, because he was *unaware* of what he was creating in such a state of despair. I think people should read it to realize that maybe whatever you want to do or create has some value, even if it isn't possible to see it in the moment. Sort of like this plant and how me looking at it made us start chatting. Maybe in ancient times this was a rare plant that only emperors and princes had, but over time anybody with a plot of land could now have it. What would that original gardener think? Would he or she know that the plant he created would be in thousands of homes, or like this book, be in the hands of millions?"

She laughs and apologizes for talking too much. I am not laughing because I am both smitten by her and reminded of my friend John. The night before, standing in a blanket of shadow and formless bodies I met Ayano, who was like a beacon of light in a maelstrom. Tonight, this girl, this girl named—

"I'm sorry, what's your name?" I ask.

"Winona," she replies with a smile.

Tonight, this girl named Winona meets me in darkness again, this time surrounded by life and plants, moonlight and a complete absence of alcohol. For a few minutes I puff myself up somewhat, chatting about my life interests and trying to match her anecdotes with a few of mine. For reasons I cannot fathom, she is quite happy to sit with me in the garden and talk. She asks me to get some beers and I head into the melee of the Barbeque, where all the focused garbage collecting energy of the day has now turned into raucous laughter, eating and drinking. A red-faced Ayano is sitting with Bill and his girlfriend and one of the guys from my training group, a cherubic guy with a frizzy shock of blonde hair named Kansas. No one really notices me as I fish two cans of Asahi from an igloo pregnant with beers and head back into the garden. Winona and I have several beers as she chats about her journeys through Asia, America and Africa, sojourns of blistering heat, random encounters and stories of being lost in dangerous areas. I wasn't drinking much, but had morphed from my bumbling moody earlier self into someone completely aware.

"Let's go to the beach," she says to me. "I always like walking there in the night when I am here."

She chuckles and grabs my hand as we head out the back gate. The bright moonlight shows her rosy cheeks, and I can see that she's a little drunk, but enjoying herself. She runs ahead of me, across the road towards the trees, and I look back, thinking of Ayano at the table, red-faced and oblivious to my absence. I follow Winona.

Our feet crunch on the sand and the sound echoes throughout the trees. Moonlight lights our way throughout the darkness. She holds my hand again, firmly this time and we come to an opening in the forest, blistering with brightness. The sky above is brightly lit, wrapped in a belt of puffy clouds beneath a shining moon sheathed a semi-circular arch. Breathtaking, I think. Maybe these are the moments, moments in light where shadows hide. Blue moonbeams cover the surface of the leaves around us.

"Sit," Winona beckons.

From some secret location, she produces a bottle of whiskey.

"I'm a bad girl!" she says with a laugh, popping the cork. She takes a heavy sip while holding my eyes in direct contact then extends the bottle to me. Drinking the burning liquid feels strange, as I am intoxicated with something else. I still cannot see the sea because of the trees around me but I can hear it, waves in full chorus, playing with the sand. The ocean breeze caresses my body like a thousand hands.

"This is what living is all about," Winona says.

The beauty of the ocean and the moon and this unusual girl beside me overwhelms me. We drink and bask in the mutual bliss of the moment, without speaking for some time. She bounces upwards in a smooth rapid motion, displaying an athleticism I didn't notice before. She smiles and gestures for me to come to her, before running into the trees at a full clip. I pause, unsure of what to do. This is not a life I have ever lived, laying on moonlit forest grounds chasing beautiful women through trees. My face is warm from the whiskey and I look around for her, but she has vanished. I hear nothing. I go forward and left, to where I think she might have run. Small tree branches scratch me playfully and I notice wherever I am the trees are quite dense, unlike the sparse patches I'd walked through earlier in the day. Trees surround me and I know I'm lost.

I'm in a thicket, completely illuminated by bright slivers of moonlight with thick-trunked trees as a captive audience. Uneven mounds of sand sleep in basins of shadow. A low, moaning wind echoes now in the distance and I feel heat rising from my toes through the hairs on my shin upwards to my groin and stomach. Obvious things do not hold their usual clarity. I knew the moon was above me, somewhere, but I could not see it anymore. All around me objects feel pregnant in their proximity. Trees and leaves touch my skin in electric shocks though they are some distance away. I feel the presence of someone else nearby, emanating an intoxicating, predatory energy. My heart flutters like a blanket caught in a high wind.

My steps are slow and muddled, my heartbeat thunder. The familiar sky has left me like a dishonest wife, and it was just I, the trees, the sand and that thick, heavy presence. Heaving through the sand as I near the trees I see her. She is illuminated by a sole beam of light, her skin blue veined and near translucent, the abstruse silhouette of her giant bow a nightmare. All the while, the heat increases in my body. Fat drops of moisture form on my forehead, under my neck and around my lips. Water screams to leave my body and the sand, cool before, feels hot and jagged, less friendly. As I step closer to her I become more inflamed with desire, my penis pressing hard against my jeans, the sensations around me rippling in a panoply of colors. She does not move, remaining a dark outline, her intentions a dark whisper. They say ghosts cannot speak, and she did not. The chaos around me stops, and the moon is gone. All is silence and darkness. I let out a muffled scream as her face appears from the shadows like a submarine emerging from underwater, her mouth wide and open, voiceless. I feel that mind boggling sexual energy again, the heat and wetness on my body strange. A cold dead hand gestures for me to follow her and I am powerless to resist. Black shadows and dark sand greet me for a few minutes, until I feel the wind again and smell the sea. She is still some distance away, the Ribbon lady, her massive bow billowing like a sail in the wind. The moon is also back, painting the swirling sand light blue as I trudge forward in heavy steps. She goes a few steps into the water, disappearing slowly as it reaches her waist. Turning around to face me, I see that the bangs over her eyes are gone, her eyes now startlingly real, blistering with intensity. Everything in me wants whatever she has to offer but I can barely move, my feet like cement blocks. I surge forward, towards her and the blackness of the sea as she goes deeper and deeper into its depths. I can sense it is no longer just the sea that I am being drawn to. The wind is angry and slaps me with weighty pockets of sand and spray. I cannot see a horizon line, only a black mirror with no reflection. The lady with the ribbon is deeper into the black, drawing me to her.

Waist high, neck high she goes in. As the first pinch of the sea's icy grip clenches my ankles when I step in, I erupt in an orgasm that shakes me to my core. White light spins around my eyes and I fall backwards, in a heap onto the wet sand, convulsing. A hand like stone grabs my ankle, pulling me forward with incredible strength. I look down between my legs, first seeing only the obsidian sea snarling at me with froth and foam, then her head emerges; the woman with the Ribbon, her eyes white and teeth bared, hissing in unison with the sea. The massive Ribbon on her head ripples as if it has a life of its own, gesticulating and wobbling in an odd rhythm. She pulls me into the water while I kick and scream, her hand on my ankle like fire. A surge drags me deeper, sprinkling shards of icy sensations across my chest. The cold gray face keeps bobbing up and down in the water, all the while the hand stays firm on my leg, pulling me under inch by inch. Water is coming into my mouth now and I sputter like a child at their first swimming lesson. I see nothing save the black sky and sea around me, with glimpses of the moon ravaged by salt burning my eyes. The grip is tight and firm, and water starts to enter my nose. I scream but nothing comes out of my mouth. My fingers stretch towards the moonlight and its promise of light and love. I kick hard and feel the hand let go, my eyes never leaving the moon as I ease myself back onto shore, panting.

I am not sure how long I lay there, but when I come to, Winona is standing over me. Her hair hangs over her face in shadow, a dark mask. Then she faces me, the light of the moon showing her kind smile.

"There you are," she says wistfully.

I laugh with relief, the moonlit beach bright and welcoming, the black sea now a forgotten memory. I sit up and she comes beside me and we watch the horizon, both of us strangers on the verge of a path to something else. We look at the infinity of the sea and are also looking the infinity within ourselves.

"Are you okay?" she asks, her perky eyes filled with concern.

"I am now," I say, standing up.

I hold her hand and we walk back into the woods, towards Bill's house.

ABOUT THE AUTHOR

Marcus Bird is a writer, filmmaker and musician from Kingston, Jamaica. He is author of four books; *Kingston Nights, Naked as The Day, Sex, Drugs & Jerk Chicken* and his short story collection *An Elephant In Kingston: And other stories.*

Questions? E-mail Marcus at: marcusbird@gmail.com

ALSO BY **MARCUS BIRD**

KINGSTON NIGHTS

In a Kingston where every night you compete for the attention of young women with world famous athletes, reggae superstars and millionaire businessmen, a young promoter named Indie battles with traumatic issues from the past while trying to stay afloat in the choking social atmosphere of endless parties and casual hookups. As he falls deeper into a growing malaise, he meets a girl who seems to be his only salvation out of the Kingston fishbowl. Or is she? Kingston Nights takes us into a dark, edgy modern day Jamaica far removed from quaint beaches, all-inclusive hotels and countryside hideaways.

SEX, DRUGS and JERK CHICKEN

Three completely different young men find themselves in the sex-fueled, emotionally vacant backdrop of nighttime Washington D.C, as they search for meaning in a series of events that force them to deal with loss, love and question it all. Sex, Drugs and Jerk Chicken takes us headfirst into a view of a version of American culture we don't always see but have probably heard about; sex with strangers, heiresses who like boy toys, insecurity eclipsed by alcohol, all seen through the lens of life in a big city.

Naked As The Day

A young man finds himself in ragingly cosmopolitan Tokyo, haunted by memories of the past, facing an uncertain future. When a typical twenty-something year old English teacher in Japan develops severe physical and psychological aversions to his daily routine in a small town, he decides to move to Tokyo with a few months worth of savings in search of more stimulating horizons. As his physical symptoms remain, and now hit with the demands that come with living in one of the world's most expensive cities, he must take a fast track course in both survival and self-actualization from a host of characters including libidinous transients, self-proclaimed celebrities and kleptomaniac supermodels. Armed with few skills in the face of an uncertain future, Naked As The Day takes us on an occasionally humorous and poignant journey of human choices and ultimately, their consequences.

BOOKS AVAILABLE ON AMAZON

www.ingramcontent.com/pod-product-compliance
Lightning Source LLC
Chambersburg PA
CBHW020647180626
46816CB00003B/1165